MW00759912

"You won't want to close your eyes in a hospital ever again. Dr. Perry Miller has obviously seen what happens when surgical patients are unconscious, and when they stay that way. What a treat when a leading doctor has such a knack for literal heart-pounding story telling.

"Don't read this book before you go to a hospital. Sure it's comforting when an anesthesiologist like Dr. Perry Miller writes that anesthesia is no more dangerous than driving to the hospital, but driving can be dangerous. Accidents happen on the road and in a surgical suite but sometimes, as in *Lethal Injection*, it might not be an accident at all. It is fascinating when a top medical expert combines medical expertise with powerful and entertaining writing skills to open the door to aspects of medicine patients never see.

"Dr. Perry Miller's combination of medical expertise with captivating story telling skills introduces the reader of *Lethal Injection* to what could be the next Michael Crichton.

"The term heart pounding fiction gets overused. However, in *Lethal Injection* an anesthesiologist startles his readers by describing the actual heart pounding that takes place during surgery when the person on the operating table suddenly flatlines. Dr. Perry Miller takes his readers on a medical roller coaster of a mystery that is difficult to put down, with an authenticity that should earn readers at least a couple of medical school credits."

—HARVEY SCHWARTZ, author of *Never Again*

"This medical thriller begins with the most powerful man in Boston's entire medical establishment dying of cardiac arrest in the OR while under the care of Dr. Lucy Rivera, anesthesiologist. Foul play is suspected, and Lucy's husband, Dr. Gideon Lowell takes charge, intent on proving his wife's innocence in spite of the police warning him off. The twists and turns of the case keep you turning page after page as the tension builds, and the well-crafted surprises will delight any and all mystery lovers. Perry Miller has created a story that is shocking and suspenseful, and will make you seek out a second, and perhaps a third opinion, before ever signing up for cardiac surgery."

—JOHN J. JESSOP, author of *Pleasuria: Take as Directed, Guardian Angel: Unforgiven,* and *Guardian Angel: Indoctrination*

"A fun book. The reader learns a lot about medicine and computers in a very readable story. It's no small feat to weave medical terminology through a drama, but as they say in gymnastics, Perry Miller nailed the landing."

"Medical mysteries are somewhat bewildering and trusting today's medical establishment can be even more terrifying. Especially when healthy patients die. Dr. Perry Miller paints a horrifying image of just such a tale in his new novel, *Lethal Injection*. Somewhere between corruption and cover up, Dr. Miller brings to light a hidden agenda no normal person would agree to tackle. Within these pages, readers will begin to question what is truth and what is fiction. A frightening but realistic read."

"*Lethal Injection* is reminiscent of an enjoyable classic Sam Spade murder mystery with a medical twist. 'Paging Dr. Gumshoe, you're needed in the OR stat!'

"In the spirit of Sam Spade, Dr. Gideon Lowell sets out to discover who is trying to frame his wife for a murder that occurred in an operating room. It is no easy task in the hospital's high stress environment which is a maze of high stakes intrigue. Motivations abound when big egos collide amid the hospital's takeover and result in backstabbing, sabotage and subterfuge. All the confusing symptoms of villainy could lead to multiple suspects, but the good Doctor is shrewd and calculating with a swashbuckling whatever-it-takes attitude. If he can outwit a 'don't mess with my case' detective who has him in his cross hairs, he might be able to solve this deadly case."

Lethal Injection

by Perry Miller

Published by

 köehlerbooks™

210 60th Street
Virginia Beach, VA 23451
800–435–4811
www.koehlerbooks.com

LETHAL INJECTION

PERRY MILLER

VIRGINIA BEACH
CAPE CHARLES

1

There is no hard and fast rule saying when to stop trying to resuscitate someone who has had a cardiac arrest. More than twenty minutes with no electrical activity in the heart is one rule of thumb, and it appeared that we were way past that.

Thirty minutes earlier, I had been across town sitting in a lecture hall at Boston Central Hospital. A friend of mine was giving a talk about treating patients with stroke. The talk was almost over when my cell phone started vibrating, yanking me out of a very relaxing daydream about the Florida Keys.

I didn't recognize the number, but it said *Laurel Hill Hospital.* That was where my wife was working. I silenced it. If Lucy wanted something, she would text. It was much less intrusive. A few seconds later, my cell vibrated again. Same number. I silenced it once again, but I had the feeling that this was a lost cause. I was right. It immediately vibrated a third time. Lucy wouldn't do this.

I pushed my way to the nearest aisle and headed out to the hall.

"Hi. This is Dr. Gideon Lowell. What's the problem?"

One of the anesthesia technicians who worked with my wife answered, "Your wife needs you here right now. It's an emergency."

I felt a momentary jolt of adrenaline.

"Where is she?" I asked. "What's the emergency?"

"She's in the operating room. Her patient had a cardiac arrest."

This was very strange.

"Why does she need me?"

"I have no idea. She just said you should come right away."

What was I supposed to do if Lucy's patient arrested on the operating table? There were plenty of people there to help her.

I was an ER doc at Boston Central Hospital. Lucy worked there too as an anesthesiologist. Our whole health system was in the process of taking over Laurel Hill Community Hospital where Lucy was working for a few months to help out. I wasn't sure I was even allowed to touch patients there.

"Tell her I'll be there as soon as I can. Maybe twenty minutes." I headed out to the street and flagged down a cab.

"Go as fast as you can. It's a medical emergency," I said for the first time in my life. It seemed to work in the movies. The cabbie took me literally and we spent the next fifteen minutes careening around on the notoriously twisting streets of Greater Boston. On the one hand I felt like telling him to slow down for God's sake, but on the other hand he was just following instructions. He ran two red lights and nosed out at least five cars at various intersections. I was impressed. I gave him forty dollars for an eighteen-dollar fare.

Laurel Hill had the gracious feel of an upscale suburban hospital even though it was not that far from downtown. I'd been there several times visiting Lucy when she was on call. I walked rapidly through the entrance, spotted a staircase, and dashed up four flights. I was panting by the time I got to the top. The OR suite was just down the hall, and that's where things got really weird. Four men in dark suits stood in the hallway looking distracted and upset. They were huddled in a group with their backs to the OR holding area. One of the doors swung open, and I could see several patients on stretchers waiting to be rolled in for surgery.

All four men were talking anxiously into cell phones, and I recognized two of them with a shock. One was the chief operating officer of the entire health system, and the other was the Laurel Hill Hospital chief of staff. *What are they doing here?* I walked quickly into the men's locker room, changed into surgical scrubs so I'd be allowed inside the OR area, and continued out into the corridors of the main OR suite.

The anesthesia tech who called me was waiting. He led me down a corridor into a long, narrow scrub room that separated two operating rooms. Plate-glass windows gave me a clear view of both rooms.

OK. Here I am.

Now I had to figure out why.

On one side of me was peace and quiet. A patient was asleep on the operating table. Two surgeons, slightly bent over, were doing something inside the patient's abdomen. As I watched, a surgeon reached out and a nurse placed an instrument softly into his hand. Looking into that operating room was restful and serene.

In total contrast, the operating room on the other side of the narrow scrub room was in chaos. Any pretense at sterility had long since been abandoned. At least ten people were busily doing things in different parts of the room. Paper boxes and plastic wrap, which once held drugs, IV tubing, and equipment, were scattered all over the floor. It was a familiar mess. This was what a cardiac arrest frequently looked like.

A man's body lay on the operating table, totally exposed. His skin was almost as white as a Greek statue with the slightest tinge of blue. Light-green drapes, once carefully arranged around the surgical site, now hung off the operating table onto the floor. The man's abdomen was a sickly orange where it had been painted with antiseptic solution. His chest was covered with light-gray hair, some of which was dry and curly. The rest was plastered down with glop that had been smeared on during what must have been multiple attempts to get his heart going again.

The resuscitation had clearly been going on for some time, and nothing seemed to be working. A surgeon was administering chest compressions. As I watched, he stepped back as another doctor placed defibrillator paddles on each side of the patient's heart. "Clear!" They shocked him to no avail. As far as I could tell, peering at the EKG from the scrub room, the patient's heart was flatline.

Lucy stood by the patient's head, wearing blue surgical scrubs and a soft paper face mask, her long dark hair tucked up into a light-blue paper cap. I watched as she squeezed a black rubber bag attached to the anesthesia machine, presumably passing 100 percent oxygen into the patient's lungs through an endotracheal tube. She looked composed and in control. There was clearly nothing I could do to help her, and I still had no idea why I was there.

From the sidelines, it was pretty clear that this resuscitation was going nowhere, and it was probably time to start calling it to a close. Lucy glanced up and saw me. She held out a hand, telling me not to move. Then, breaking eye contact with me, she turned both hands upwards as if she was asking someone up there, "How the hell did this happen?"

One of the masked figures standing beside her looked up, spoke to her briefly, and then came out into the scrub room and removed his mask. It was Dave Freeman, one of Lucy's fellow anesthesiologists.

"What's going on?" I asked.

He looked at me strangely. "Nobody told you?"

"Nobody told me anything. Lucy just said I had to come here right away. I have no idea what this is all about."

Freeman shook his head, half turning to look back into the OR.

"You see that man in there?" He pointed to the operating table. "That's James Arnold."

"You mean *the* James Arnold? The CEO of our health system?"

"Yes, that James Arnold."

The most powerful and perhaps the most feared man in Boston's entire medical establishment had just had a cardiac arrest. On my wife's operating table. Under her care.

This was not good.

2

t was another ten minutes before the surgeon finally announced it was time to stop. By then the resuscitation must have been going on for at least an hour, which was not at all unusual. I wondered if Arnold had been flatline all that time.

As if someone had flipped a switch, all the activity suddenly stopped, and people started wandering out of the room. In the meantime, I had decided that Lucy must have called me here so she would have somebody to talk to about what just happened.

What do I say? You do the best you can, but sometimes bad things happen? It's not your fault? No, Lucy didn't need platitudes. I had to know more if I was going to contribute something useful and intelligent.

It was difficult when any patient died, but usually the patient was elderly or very sick, or both, and death was not unexpected. This was different. James Arnold was in the prime of life; this was something the entire Boston medical community would want to hear about and gossip about ad nauseam.

I stepped into the OR. Lucy looked up and began walking over to join me. Then she suddenly stopped and turned. Two nurses were cleaning up. She ran over and grabbed hold of them.

"Stop. Stop. You can't do that. Leave everything just the way it is."

Both nurses froze, startled and confused. Lucy took each of them by the arm and led them out of the room—pulled them out, really. When they were gone, she turned back to me.

"I need your help." There was a tremor in her voice.

I walked over and placed my hand gently on her shoulder and kept it there. I had a lot of questions that would have to wait.

"Take a deep breath," I said.

She slowly took three. Then she reached up and put her hand on top of mine and just stood there for a moment.

One more breath and she was ready to talk.

"Listen, Gideon, at this point I'm not even thinking straight. You're the patient safety expert. You have to help me figure this out."

She was referring to the medical school's Patient Safety Committee. I was a member. The goal was to structure patient care in ways that kept patients as safe as possible. We were clearly way past that here.

I guess Lucy could tell what I was thinking.

"Look, you like solving problems," she said. "You're good at it. We really need that here." She paused, looking at me. "*I* really need that here. That's why I had them get you here in the first place."

OK, that makes sense. Now at least I knew why I was here. Of course, I still didn't know what the problem was that I was supposed to solve.

"I'll do the best I can," I said. "Where do I start?"

She looked around the room. "First of all, we can't let people clean up. They're going to try. The body needs to stay here, too."

"Why, Lucy? What's going on?"

I was searching her face for some kind of clue. Clearly, I was missing something.

"That's James Arnold." She gestured toward the operating table. "Did anyone tell you that?"

"Yes, I know. Freeman told me."

"This was a simple, straightforward gallbladder operation. There's no way this should have happened. Arnold plays tennis tournaments. I've seen pictures of his office. He has trophies all over the place. He was very fit."

She was right. With a healthy patient, the risks of anesthesia were about the same as the risks of riding in a car. What happened here was the equivalent of a car accidentally driving off a cliff.

I needed to help her settle down, but I had no idea where to start. I struggled to come up with something to say.

"So maybe he had medical problems that nobody knew about. What do you think?"

Lucy didn't reply. She had a distant expression in her eyes. Now that it was all over, her mind was trying to process everything that had happened.

I waited for her to return. Her blank stare gradually faded.

"OK, so what about heart disease?" I asked. "Does he have heart disease?"

"Yes, he has heart disease," she nodded and then paused. "No," she said finally, contradicting herself. "Arnold *used* to have heart disease. He had a triple bypass two years ago. His heart was fixed. He was in his mid-fifties; he played tennis tournaments. He won tennis tournaments, for crying out loud."

The surgeon who had been administering chest compressions had been listening and now walked over to join us.

"What do you think happened?" He looked just about as stunned as Lucy. He hadn't had a chance to do anything but prep and drape, and now his patient was dead. He had been pumping up and down on Arnold's chest for an hour or more trying to bring him back to life.

He looked quizzically at me. He clearly had no idea who I was. I reached out and shook his hand.

"I'm Gideon Lowell. I work in the ER at Boston Central Hospital. Lucy's my wife."

"John Russo," he said absently, shaking my hand.

I had never met Russo and knew nothing about him. The stereotype of a surgeon was tall, thin, and athletic. Russo was around five feet eight with a medium-sized paunch and five o'clock shadow despite the fact that it was still early morning. If you passed him in the street, you might think he ran the neighborhood deli.

But he radiated an aura of quiet competence, and I knew he had to be good. Arnold would know who to pick as his surgeon. Arnold was a surgeon himself and still did a little surgery here at Laurel Hill.

Well, actually, not anymore. I looked over at the body.

Still dead.

I've seen plenty of dead people, but the sight of death still gives me the creeps. Arnold's body was just lying there—nude except for a few surgical drapes hanging off onto the floor. His eyes were taped shut to keep them from drying out. No longer a big concern. An endotracheal tube was sticking up out of his mouth, like a lonely stalk of celery in a Bloody Mary.

Death came in many forms. Arnold's had come quickly and refused to relinquish its hold.

"Hey, Gideon. Focus. You need to help me out here." Lucy pulled my arm.

I shook my head and tuned back in.

"The patient went flatline at the very start of the case," she said, talking to both of us but looking mostly at me. "There was no warning at all. At first, I thought the EKG had disconnected. Then I listened to his heart. There was nothing. No heartbeat. No pulse. Nothing."

"What happened then?" I asked.

"She called me over," Russo said. "I listened to his heart. I felt for a pulse. But like Lucy says, there was nothing."

"So, we started CPR," they said virtually in unison.

Russo rubbed his hands together, looking around the room. "This is crazy."

"Could the tube have been in his esophagus?" I asked. This was like asking Lucy if she was a total incompetent, but it was the next logical question.

Lucy shook her head. "He wasn't even intubated. I had just induced anesthesia. Then I gave him vecuronium. I was ventilating by mask, waiting for it to take effect so I could intubate. That's when the EKG went flatline."

"It was the very beginning of the case." Russo nodded. "We were waiting for Lucy to tell us we could start. That's when he arrested."

"His oxygenation was fine," Lucy added.

"So, what went wrong? Could he have gotten an electric shock, maybe, or something like that?" I was grasping at straws.

"I think it was something he got intravenously," Lucy said. "Take a look at his arm."

She pulled back one of the drapes and we looked at the IV in

Arnold's left forearm. A pale reddish streak ran up to his elbow, outlining the vein where the IV fluid had flowed in.

"That sure doesn't look normal." I was stating the obvious.

"You better believe that's not normal," Russo said. He looked at Lucy. "What could have caused that?"

I studied the red mark and started thinking about different things you might inject if you wanted to kill someone.

"Well, the first thing that comes to my mind is potassium," Lucy said. "I'm pretty sure potassium could inflame a vein like that. And a bolus of potassium would obviously stop the heart."

"So, you think he somehow got potassium?" Russo seemed dubious. "I mean, how?"

"I have no idea," Lucy said. "What else could it be? Epinephrine? But I don't think epinephrine would do this to a vein. Maybe. Who knows?"

She looked back at the vein as if searching for a clue.

Then she continued. "I put that IV in myself and the only person who gave him anything through it was me."

I was still trying to imagine what might have been injected through the IV, and for some reason, the concept of battery acid got stuck in my mind. "Does it have to be something medical? I mean, what about battery acid?"

Russo and Lucy both gave me a funny look.

"Gideon!" Lucy said, shaking her head. I knew what she was thinking. *Gideon, you're thinking way too far outside the box . . . again.* But she was used to it. I made her read a whole bunch of books about attention deficit disorder before she married me.

"I mean just as an example," I persisted. "There must be a whole lot of nonmedical things that could do that."

"Who knows?" she said finally. "And you're right; we have no idea. It could be anything at all."

"So, you think potassium somehow got into that syringe?" Russo said.

"I don't know," Lucy said. "Can you think of something else?"

"But how could it? I mean, how did it get there?" I said.

"I drew up the syringe," Lucy said slowly, clearly thinking back to the start of the case. "I took the vecuronium from a new

bottle that was clearly labelled. I broke the metal seal myself."
She rummaged around in the top drawer of the anesthesia cart
looking for the bottle and finally pulled it out.

"In any case, there's no potassium anywhere in this room,"
she said. "We only use it for hearts, and all the heart rooms are
way down at the other end of the hall. We use potassium there
when we deliberately stop the heart to go on bypass."

Russo suddenly moved in closer. "Look where the label is."

"What do you mean?" Lucy asked.

Russo pointed at the anesthesia cart where several syringes
containing different drugs were sitting side by side.

"All those other syringes have their labels stuck on halfway
down the barrel, right next to the little scale that tells you how
much you are injecting. The label on the vecuronium syringe is
on the opposite side of the barrel from the scale."

Lucy looked at the other syringes. "I always stick the label
right next to the scale. It lets me see the name of the drug and
how much I'm giving at the same time. It helps prevent mistakes."

We looked at each other, realizing the same thing at the
same time.

"You know what that means." Lucy held up the vecuronium
syringe. "This is not the syringe I drew up." She put it back down on
the cart gingerly, almost as if she were setting down a loaded gun.

"Oh my God." Now she was looking at me.

"So, someone switched the syringe?" Russo said. "Took your
syringe and replaced it with one that looked exactly the same
but with the label in a slightly different place?"

Lucy looked at me. "That is definitely not the syringe I drew
up. But it was sitting right where I had put my syringe."

We all paused for a moment, processing.

"We should have it tested," I said. "We need to know what's
in it."

"That's a good point." Lucy's voice was now tinged with a
touch of urgency. "We should have someone run tests on all
these syringes. And on the bottles I drew the drugs up from. We
need to know what they all actually contain."

"Was the room ever empty after you drew up the drugs and
put them out here?" I asked.

"Let me think," Lucy said. "Surgery was scheduled to start at seven thirty. I got here early and had everything all set up maybe forty-five minutes ahead of time. That would be six forty-five. Then I left the room to get ready to meet Arnold in the holding area. The nurses must have begun setting up all their stuff sometime after I left. So, the room might have been empty for maybe ten or fifteen minutes. We brought Arnold in around seven twenty."

I remembered my days in medical school. Anesthesiologists left syringes all drawn up sitting around in empty ORs all the time. Even overnight—ready for an emergency that might be rushed up to the OR in the middle of the night. The last thing you wanted to do was draw up drugs in a hurry while a critical patient was being wheeled into the door.

"Murder," Russo said abruptly, snapping me out of my reverie. "We're talking about murder."

We all looked at each other as this realization fully sank in. Murder was indeed what we had been talking about, but saying the word brought the reality home.

I thought for a moment. I had never heard of anything like this happening anywhere before.

"If this was murder, that makes this room a crime scene," I said.

"Yes, it does," Lucy agreed. None of us spoke. We just looked at each other and gazed around the room.

"So, what do we do now?" Russo finally asked. "Call the police?"

It was the logical next step.

Patients died in hospitals all the time. As a doctor, you learned to accept it and move on. Calling the police was not something anyone even thought of doing when a patient died in the hospital.

Of course, this was different.

"Someone has to call the police." Lucy nodded. "And someone needs to stay here and make sure nobody tries to clean up this room." She looked at me. "I can't stay here."

"I'll stay," I said. "Where are you going?"

"I need to talk to the family."

"I do too," Russo said. "Oh my God, Dr. Arnold's wife is right down the hall in the waiting room. They're probably waiting for me to talk to her. I should go right away."

We had been standing there talking for ten or maybe fifteen minutes. Who knew what Arnold's wife had been told—if anything.

"I'll come with you if that's OK," Lucy said.

"Good idea. We'll talk to her together," Russo said.

I nodded. There was something about Russo that somehow inspired confidence. If I ever needed to be cut open, I'd be very comfortable if someone like him was holding the knife.

He paused for a moment, then continued. "But what do we tell her? I mean, we obviously need to tell her what happened. But how do we explain why?"

Lucy picked up his train of thought. "He arrested on the operating table and we don't know why. We should tell her exactly that. We did everything we could to bring him back, but nothing worked. You know, it's always possible he had a massive heart attack or a pulmonary embolism. Unlikely. But definitely possible."

"If it was anything like that, we'll find out at autopsy," Russo said. "But if we're calling the police, I need to tell her there are other aspects of what happened that we are concerned about."

"We should get someone to stay with her," Lucy said, "if she's here all alone."

We all nodded.

Russo gestured to the door. Reaching out, I squeezed Lucy's hand.

"You go talk to Arnold's wife. I'll stay here and look after this room."

"I also need to talk to Hank Strier sometime soon," she said. Strier was chief of anesthesiology at Laurel Hill Hospital. "Strier needs to know about this."

So did a whole lot of people.

3

Lucy had only been gone a couple of minutes when Hank Strier appeared. He gave me a friendly little wave as he entered the room. We had been on several medical school committees together and knew each other well.

I was glad to see him. I was starting to feel a little uncomfortable alone with Arnold's body. This was now a presumed crime scene, and I was not even on the hospital staff. I wasn't sure the hospital would care, but the police might find it odd, especially since I was Lucy's husband.

Lucy had passed Strier in the hall and filled him in. He looked at the syringes. Then he looked at Arnold's arm and ran his fingers up and down the vein. I had no idea what he might be feeling for. He probably didn't either.

"This is not normal," he said, looking at me.

I nodded.

"I'll go call security and get this started," he continued. "Would you mind staying here? I'll be right back."

So, I was alone in the room again, but at least now I had Strier's official blessing. It was still a bit creepy. I had nothing to do but stand there and not touch anything. I was surrounded by the brightly lit, pale-yellow walls of the OR. The only sound was the soft whirring of the overhead ventilation system.

Strier returned in about five minutes with Dave Freeman, Lucy's fellow anesthesiologist. They were a mismatched pair—Freeman tall and thin, Strier short and a bit chubby.

"OK," Strier said, "hospital security is coming and police detectives are on their way. They're all going to need to change into scrubs to get in here, and we'll obviously have to close down this room. We'll also close the room next door as soon as that case is finished. I just hope we can keep the rest of the schedule going."

Strier started to pull Lucy's stool away from the operating table, intending to sit down. He abruptly stopped and pulled back his hands.

"Whoops. I forgot this is a crime scene. I guess we should leave."

That seemed like a good idea.

"What do you think? Can we keep the rest of the ORs open?" Strier asked Freeman as we walked out to the scrub room. I tried to imagine what we would do if something like this happened in the emergency room. Clearly, we couldn't just shut everything down.

"I don't know," Freeman said. "If there's a nut on the loose—" He paused, letting his thought sort of hang out there in midair. "I mean, what about all the drugs that are drawn up in the other operating rooms? What if someone is running around substituting drugs all over the place? We're going to look like idiots if any more patients start having cardiac arrests."

Strier clearly didn't want to think about that. With a fleeting look of panic he glanced at Dave and then back at me. "Fine. Enough said. But we need concrete ideas. What specifically do we do?" he asked Freeman.

"You got me," Freeman said. "This is uncharted territory."

He was right. I was pretty sure no hospital had a nut-on-the-loose-in-the-OR protocol that told us exactly what to do.

"OK," Strier said, wiping a few beads of sweat off his forehead. "But, for example, if we close down all the ORs, when do we open them again? It could be weeks before we ever find out what happened here. We may never know for sure."

"Let's not go crazy here, Hank," Freeman said. "All the other rooms are up and running fine."

"Good point, Dave. That's a really good point. But we still need to take all the precautions we can think of."

"All right, here's one idea," Freeman said. "We could have everybody draw up new drugs from new bottles. And tell them not to leave syringes full of drugs alone in an empty room between cases."

"Right, good idea. Let's do that. What else?"

Freeman thought some more. "What about collecting all the vecuronium? Even all the unopened bottles, and tell everybody to use a different muscle relaxant."

"Sure. Why not?" Strier agreed. "We'll collect it all—the syringes and the vecuronium—and store it somewhere. I'll ask the police what to do with it. What else?" He turned to Freeman. "As you so eloquently stated, for all we know we may be dealing with a nut on the loose."

I had an idea.

"Why don't you have the hospital station people at all the entrances to the OR area and ID everybody who comes in or out? Is that possible?" We had security all around the emergency room. It seemed like they could do something like that here.

"Yes, I think the nurses could do that," Strier said. "They could keep a list—everybody who goes in and out and when. They could assign OR staff to do it. People who know almost everyone by sight. I'll talk to nursing and see what they think."

"We could write a paper about this," Freeman said. A totally off-the-wall comment as far as I was concerned, but he sounded serious. My initial reaction was to roll my eyes up and think, *Oh, come on. Please. Spare me this.* Then again, he had a point.

But Strier was clearly annoyed.

"David, no way are you going to write a paper about this."

"Why not? If something like this ever happens again somewhere, it would be good to have guidelines."

Like I said, he had a point.

"David, if you ever write a paper about this, I will personally kill you." Strier sounded like he was scolding a child. "Come on. Enough. This is not funny."

"Sorry, Hank." Freeman sounded mildly contrite, but I had a sneaking suspicion that he was going to wind up writing that paper and probably getting it published. Somewhere.

Strier didn't respond. Instead he walked past us down the length of the scrub room, opened the door to the hall, and looked out. Nothing yet. No hospital security, no uniformed police, no detectives.

"What's taking them so long?" He looked back at us. "Look, we don't all three have to babysit this room. I'll stay here until security arrives. Dave, you and Gideon go around to all the ORs. Tell everybody to draw up new drugs from unopened bottles. Tell them everything we just talked about. And keep an eye out for anything funny or unusual."

As we headed off, Strier called after us, "Don't dawdle. We need to get this done right away."

For the next fifteen minutes, Freeman and I followed instructions. I stayed outside in the various scrub rooms while he went in and talked briefly to whoever was giving anesthesia in each OR. While he did that, I looked around for anything "funny or unusual." The only catch was I didn't work in an OR, so I had no idea what to look for. In any case, I didn't see anything worth reporting.

"I assume Lucy told you what's going on here," Dave said as we started walking around. "I mean about our takeover of this department."

"Just in general terms."

"It's not good. There's a lot of bad feeling here."

Taking over the anesthesia department was just a small part of what was going on. Boston Central Health System was absorbing all of Laurel Hill Community Hospital. Lucy, Strier, Freeman, and I all worked for Boston Central Hospital, the academic teaching hospital that served as the hub of the health system. We were also all on the faculty of the medical school. The three of them had been sent to Laurel Hill to facilitate the transition of the anesthesia department.

Transition was actually a polite term for what was happening. *Hostile takeover* was more like it. A lot of the Laurel Hill medical staff were being forced out.

"For example, that was Alan Mason in there," Freeman said, gesturing to the OR he had just left. "He's just out of anesthesia residency and he's not fitting in well at all. He got here less than a year ago and he'll be let go in a few months when his contract runs out. He just bought a house a few blocks away so he could walk to work. He's extremely bitter."

I glanced back into the room, but all I could see was a thin figure in scrubs wearing a cap and mask sitting near the patient's head. He was wearing glasses, so I couldn't see any of his face.

Freeman was about to enter another OR when he pulled me aside and spoke almost in a whisper. "This next one's Namrata. Lucy must have told you about her."

"Lucy did tell me about Namrata. Just talking about Namrata makes Lucy very angry."

"Namrata has been here for about three years. She is fine clinically, but she has a terrible attitude. She doesn't seem to care about any of the people she works with. I sometimes wonder if there's something missing in her brain."

"I gather they had some kind of fight?"

"Yes, Lucy's had a couple of knockdown, drag-out, screaming catfights with Namrata. It's funny, I've known Lucy for five years. I've never seen her lose her temper once. Before Namrata, that is."

"I've never seen Lucy really lose it. Never ever. I find it hard to imagine."

I was trying to process the term "catfight." When two men got angry at each other nobody ever called it a "dogfight." Did they? Whatever.

Once we finished our whirlwind tour of the ORs, Freeman led me to the anesthesia break room, located just off the main OR corridor. This was apparently the next stop on our tour. It contained a couch, a few comfortable armchairs, and a coffee table covered with random magazines, all old and tattered. On a counter was an empty coffee machine.

"That's the famous coffee machine," Freeman informed me.

"What do you mean?"

"Lucy didn't tell you?"

I thought for a moment. "No, Lucy never said anything about a coffee machine."

"About a month after we got here, someone put something in the coffee. Strier, Lucy, and I all drank it and spent the rest of the morning suffering the consequences."

"Consequences?"

"Explosive diarrhea." He laughed.

"You're kidding."

"I'm definitely not kidding."

"I remember Lucy saying something about being sick one day, but she never said anything about coffee." I couldn't help but laugh. "Somehow I don't think that's a real medical term."

I've heard of projectile vomiting, which is a real medical term.

"Maybe not, but we all had it. The three of us. Everyone else must have known not to drink the coffee. We figured that out the next day."

"I guess that's why the machine is empty now? Nobody drinks it anymore?"

"No. Everyone still uses it. Just not the three of us. Now everything I eat or drink up here comes directly from machines in the main OR break room."

Dave walked over to a cork bulletin board mounted on the rear wall of the room and gave me a funny look as if he was not exactly sure what to say.

"How about this bulletin board? Did Lucy ever say anything about that?"

Lucy had said something about a bulletin board.

"Is that where they found the sock?" I asked.

"Yes. Did she tell you the whole story? A couple of weeks ago, someone tacked one of Lucy's socks up here along with a note that said it had been found in the call room bed used by one of the orthopedic residents." Freeman looked at me and shrugged. "It's like we're in junior high school. Someone must have stolen the sock out of Lucy's locker."

"How did people know it was Lucy's sock?" I asked.

"Some of her socks have unusual patterns. Distinctive. I'm sure you know that."

I did. I order them myself from a boutique in London.

"What does the surgical resident say? Does he know about this?" I asked.

"He refuses to say anything. He seems to think the whole thing is funny."

A jerk.

"Lucy told me about the sock," I said. "It really pissed her off. It was such a juvenile thing to do. She was getting really fed up with this place."

I was beginning to wonder if I had somehow been asleep at the switch. I'm not sure what I could have done about any of this, but I absolutely had to figure out how to help Lucy now.

"It may have been juvenile, but it was also . . ." Freeman struggled for the right word. "How do you say it? . . . Bullying?"

"Hostile?" I suggested.

"Yes. Hostile. It was definitely hostile. But it's also like all that teenage internet bullying you hear about. When people get attacked anonymously on the web."

"Right. And now Lucy's patient arrests on the operating table."

Freeman looked at me as the implication of what I was saying sank in.

"You're right. Boy, I really don't know what to make of that."

4

After our little tour, Freeman and I returned to Lucy's OR, or as Freeman put it, "to the scene of the crime." When we got there, we found both OR doors crisscrossed with long strips of white surgical tape. A handwritten sign was taped up on each door that said *POLICE LINE—DO NOT CROSS* in big block letters. This must have been Strier's idea, presumably a temporary measure until the police arrived with real crime scene tape. The kind you saw on TV.

One of the OR nurses stood guard outside the room. Freeman greeted her as we approached.

"Hi. Where's Strier?"

"Dr. Strier went to the main OR desk to talk to the nursing supervisor. Joan Maynard is in charge today. I'm supposed to stand here and make sure nobody goes into this room." She looked a bit stunned.

"Good," Freeman said. "Thank you for doing this. It's very important."

She leaned toward us. "I have never heard of anything like this happening. Ever."

"Me neither," Freeman said. The three of us stood there for a moment looking at each other. Then Freeman turned to me. "Let's find Strier."

I followed him down one of the OR corridors and out into the large rectangular room that served as the pre-op holding area.

It was mostly empty. Three patients were on stretchers awaiting surgery. They were presumably premedicated and appeared to be oblivious to everything that was going on.

The four men in dark suits I had seen earlier in the hall outside the holding area had multiplied into a milling crowd. There were several more men in dark suits, a hospital security guard in a green uniform, a blue-uniformed policeman with a City of Boston patch on his shoulder, and six or seven assorted OR staff. It was hard to know who was actually doing something useful and who was just rubbernecking.

A nurse with a clipboard was writing down the names of everybody going in or out of the OR suite, along with the time. Freeman and I told her we were leaving. She recognized Freeman. I had to show my ID. I was impressed. What we had discussed with Strier just a few minutes ago had already been put into action.

I heard Strier's voice coming from around the corner. He was right outside the little room where they coordinated OR activities as a whole—scheduling emergency cases, calling to bring patients down from the floors for surgery, and generally keeping track of everything going on.

Strier was talking to a nurse. Freeman waited for him to finish his sentence and then interrupted.

"Look, I'm running two rooms and I need to get back to them. Gideon and I just went to all the ORs and talked to everybody. They all know what to do."

"Fine," Strier said. "Go take care of your rooms. I'll let you know if I need any more help."

Freeman took off, leaving me alone with Strier.

"I didn't see anything unusual in any of the ORs," I said. "You told me to look."

He didn't react.

"Have you seen Lucy?" I asked.

"Lucy's not here. She got intercepted by a hospital lawyer after she talked to Arnold's wife. I think she's up in his office now. When she gets back, I assume the police detectives will want to talk to her. She's going to be tied up for quite a while."

I thought about what he said. Hospital lawyers played an

important role, but I was not always sure who they were really working for.

"Do you think she needs her own lawyer?" I asked. "The hospital lawyers always seem to focus on protecting the hospital. Do you think she needs someone to focus on protecting her?"

"I don't see why," Strier said. "She just needs to tell people what happened. If we got another lawyer involved, I think it would just confuse people. Like we have something to hide. We have nothing to hide."

I wondered if I should talk to a lawyer anyway. It would probably be good to have someone lined up who we could call if we needed to.

"Lucy's got to be pretty shaken up," I said.

"Of course she is. But the police must be used to that," Strier said. "I'm sure I'll be talking a lot to the detectives too. Explaining how everything works. Things like that. Don't worry. I'll look after Lucy."

Then he looked at me and thought for a moment. "Listen, I don't think there's anything to be gained by your hanging around. You should probably stay completely out of this. Let's try to keep things as simple as possible."

He was right. I was starting to feel like an extra wheel.

"OK. I'll go."

As I left the building, I texted Lucy to call me. I could juggle my schedule and come back any time if she wanted me to.

In the meantime, I needed to go somewhere quiet, sit, and really think this thing through. The whole place seemed to be in imminent danger of spinning out of control.

If it hadn't already done so.

5

Around one in the morning, I reached over and realized that Lucy's side of the bed was empty. I got up and went into the living room. There she was, sitting on the sofa with the lamp on, staring into space.

She was wearing a long, light-blue T-shirt that came down almost to her knees. On the back, in big black letters, it read, *MIT Men: The Odds are Good but the Goods are Odd.* I had given her one just like it when we started dating seriously in medical school ten years earlier. We were in the same class. She had paid to have more T-shirts made up over the years. Different colors, but always the same message. They wore out every year or two.

I thought it was her little way of saying that she knew that life with me would not always be the normal standard item. And that was OK with her. I thought the T-shirt was hilarious. At the same time, I didn't think I really needed to see it all the time. But it did help to remind me to try to keep things as normal as possible.

Like remembering to take out the trash. Like remembering to pay attention when she talked to me. My ADD mind tended to wander off and tune out whatever was going on around me.

I sat beside her on the couch.

"Hey, Stormy," I said softly. "What's going on?"

"Can't sleep," she mumbled, still staring out at nothing.

"Lie down. I'll rub your back."

She lay facedown on the couch and I started massaging her shoulders.

Stormy got her nickname when we first started going out. When my friends from college heard that I was seeing a girl from Puerto Rico, they somehow got the idea that she must be some kind of Latin firecracker with a stormy temperament. Of course, that was before they met her. They started teasing me about it, and Lucy and I both thought it funny. That was how Stormy got her nickname. She liked it.

If you've ever been in one of those castles in Spain and seen portraits on the wall of medieval Spanish noblewomen—tall, thin, long black hair, beautiful eyes—that's what Stormy looked like. Luciana was her real name; Lucy for short.

And she was the sweetest person you could ever meet, a naturally cheerful human being. I didn't know what it was she ever saw in me; all I could say was it seemed to work. She once said that it was the tiny pinch of geekiness that attracted her most. Six feet one, one eighty, thin, glasses, and still a bit of a nerd after all these years. She said just looking at me made her smile.

"You did nothing wrong," I said.

"My patient died."

"Patients die all the time. Everybody dies."

"Sick patients die. Old patients die. Young healthy patients don't die."

"Fifty-five isn't that young," I said. But she was right. Fifty-five was pretty young.

"Fifty-five is young."

I nodded. "Yeah, I guess so. You're right. But if this turns out to be murder—"

"I really want to know what was in that syringe."

"We'll know soon enough."

Lucy reached back and took my hand. She was still facedown on the couch. "What really pisses me off," she continued, "is that some of those Laurel Hill anesthesia dirtballs are happy this happened to me. I can tell by the way they look at each other."

"You mean they're happy Arnold died in your OR?"

"That's exactly what I mean. Some of them are very angry about what's happening at Laurel Hill and they think they can take it out on me. They think they can get away with that. It's like they think I'm weak, or vulnerable, or something."

"I wish I had known more about all this earlier. I feel like a jerk," I said.

"I'm too nice."

"Being nice is not a problem."

"I can't believe I volunteered to go over there to help out."

"You don't think one of them would have switched drugs on you?"

"They're snakes."

"They're doctors, Lucy. They're not going to start killing patients just because they're mad about something."

"You're probably right. I really can't see them doing it. But if that syringe was switched, somebody did it. Tinker Bell didn't switch that syringe."

"Being nasty and vindictive is one thing. But this . . . this is killing patients."

"Arnold wasn't just any patient. A lot of people at Laurel Hill despise him," Lucy said. "He was orchestrating the whole takeover process. If there is anyone to blame for the completely nasty way it's being done, it was Arnold."

"So, they kill Arnold and blame it on you? Is that what you're saying?"

"Exactly."

"Kill two birds with one stone?"

"Gideon, this is not funny."

Lucy was right. The Laurel Hill anesthesia department was malignant. I continued rubbing her back. It was time for her to get some sleep.

"Lucy. Lucy," I whispered in her ear, "you did nothing wrong."

"I know. I know. But what a mess. I can't stop thinking about it."

"You shouldn't try to bottle it up," I said. "The more you talk about it, the better."

"I'm all talked out."

She had spent most of the day talking to people about what happened. The police and the hospital lawyers. She was clearly exhausted.

I couldn't decide if I should keep rubbing her back and hope she'd fall asleep. Or maybe I should try to get her to talk, vocalize it so maybe she wouldn't just continue to stew about it.

I finally opted for the obvious. I got half an Ambien and a glass of water. She took the pill and I led her back to bed where I continued to rub her back. Twenty minutes later she was gently snoring, but then I couldn't get to sleep. I tossed around fitfully next to her. I suppose I was dozing off and on, and I think I had dreams about Laurel Hill, but I have absolutely no recollection of what they were all about.

Suddenly I was wide awake. I kept a little notebook with an attached night-light on my nightstand. I picked it up, switched on the light, unclipped the pencil, and wrote, I *have to figure this out myself.* Then I turned off the light, put the pad and pencil back on the nightstand, and rolled back onto my pillow.

Usually when I did this I fell back to sleep, read my little note in the morning, remembered what I had been thinking in the middle of the night, and then decided what if anything to do about it. My little trick wasn't working. I tossed and turned and fidgeted until I gave up.

I went out into the living room, turned on the light, and sat on the sofa with a full-size notebook on my lap. It was quarter to three in the morning. Annoying, but what was the alternative? It was clear that I needed to think this thing through if I was ever going to get back to sleep.

So I started out by writing a list of actors four or five lines apart down the left-hand side of the page—*Police, Lawyers, Strier,* and *Health Network.* In the center of the page I wrote *Lucy.* Then on the right-hand side of the page I wrote a list of issues—*Arnold, Coffee, Sock,* and *Takeover.* I sat back, looked at it, and started to think. Then I started drawing lines connecting the various actors and issues, and writing little notes alongside the lines.

I was trying to see who might be able to figure out what was going on. After about fifteen minutes, I concluded that nobody on that page was going to care enough, or have the time, to figure out who killed Arnold and why. Strier sure didn't have the time. The hospital lawyers would just circle their wagons to fend off potential attacks from wherever. The network was just a bunch of business people scurrying around doing their own thing. The police might figure out what had happened. But I couldn't convince myself that they would be able to put it all together. They had no intuition about clinical medicine. They wouldn't understand all the nuances of the takeover or fully grasp the generally toxic environment of the Laurel Hill anesthesia department.

So, this left me sitting there with my original brain flash. The one that woke me up. The only person who had any real chance of putting all the different pieces of this together was me. Yes, I would have to do it myself.

The next logical question was how.

I turned to a new blank page in my notebook and started drawing circles. More like ovals, really. I put a big oval at the top of the page labelled *Health Network*. Then I put two overlapping ovals further down on the left side of the page. One I labelled *BCH* (Boston Central Hospital) and the other I labeled *Med School*. I put four little stick figures in the area where those two ovals overlapped. These were Strier, Freeman, Lucy, and me. We were all faculty at the Boston Central Medical School, and we all worked for BCH. I drew an oval on the right side of the page labeled *LHCH* (Laurel Hill Community Hospital). I put Strier, Freeman, and Lucy there too. Then I drew lines connecting the network to the two hospitals. After I got all this down on the page, I sat looking at it for a little while.

The four stick figures were all medical school faculty, and all worked at BCH. In addition to this, of course, Strier, Freeman, and Lucy were over at Laurel Hill, surrounded on all sides by community doctors. Sent from the hallowed halls of academic medicine to the wide-open spaces of community practice, sort of like Wyatt Earp and his brothers being sent over to Dodge City to try to get things under control. Of course, community medicine was not the Wild West. If I ever had anything wrong with me that wasn't truly exotic, I'd go to a good community doctor every time. But I digress.

Another consideration was that I was on the patient safety committee at the medical school. We developed procedures to keep patients safe. For example, how to make sure that a unit of blood got transfused into the correct patient and never into anybody else. Or that the left kidney got removed instead of the right kidney by mistake. I sat there for a few minutes trying to imagine how any of that might translate into figuring out who switched that syringe. Maybe my subconscious could come up with an answer if I went back to sleep.

In any case, it seemed like there was something here I should be able to work with. I thought about it for a while and then put the notebook down, turned off the light, and went back to bed. This time I fell asleep, and the next thing I knew it was morning.

6

The next morning, I sent the kids in to wake Lucy up. There's nothing like having a six-year-old boy and a four-year-old girl jumping up and down all over your bed to get you in the right frame of mind to meet the day.

Lucy was on the OR schedule, so she had to leave by six thirty. It was therefore up to me to shepherd the kids out to their carpool, hopefully on time. I was doing a three-to-eleven evening ER shift and didn't have to be anywhere until mid-afternoon.

Lucy was almost always up before me, but the Ambien must have slowed her down. I went ahead and made breakfast—blueberry pancakes, which the kids loved, and turkey sausage, which at least today they ate without complaint. Lucy arrived at the table wearing her normal work clothes—sweatpants and a fresh T-shirt. This one didn't have a message on it. There was no reason to dress up. The minute she got to the hospital, the outer layer went right into a locker and was replaced by surgical scrubs.

Despite the lingering effects of the Ambien, Lucy still completed her morning task. This consisted of handing me a to-do list for the day. I like to think of Lucy as my muse, but she has to be a very organized muse.

The top half of the list were things I needed to do for work. I would add and cross things off during the day. If I forgot to type my changes into the computer, Lucy did it for me. The bottom half listed everything Lucy wanted me to do. Whenever she forgot to do this and tried to tell me something verbally, my ADD generally just let it float off into oblivion. With the list, it got done and she didn't have to say a word.

Everything that needed to be done that day was in bright red and bolded. At the very top of the page, she had put *Talk to Strier—figure out what we need to do*. In addition to being bold and red, this was in extra-large font and underlined.

I looked over the list and had a sudden idea. I was remembering the Wild West from the middle of the night.

"I think I need to be deputized," I said.

"Deputized?"

"Deputized."

"You mean like Gideon Lowell, deputy sheriff?" She smiled. I knew she was thinking, *OK, what now?*

"Yeah. Sort of."

"Then what?" She started laughing. "Then you run around arresting people?"

"No, no. But then I can run around talking to people about what happened yesterday. Right now we have police and hospital lawyers running around, and who knows who else. You and I have no idea what they are doing, and nobody's going to tell us. At least not much. We need to get a handle on this whole mess ourselves."

"OK. So how do you get deputized?" She was smiling and shaking her head.

"I think I need some kind of official-sounding mission. A semi-official role, so I can go around asking questions. And it should be as low key as possible. I think Strier is the answer. I'll see if he will ask me to start looking into this on behalf of the Department of Anesthesiology."

Since Strier and I knew each other well, I thought he'd be willing.

"Hank just needs to say that?"

"He should probably send me a one-sentence email. Without that, I am just your husband asking questions. But with an official-sounding role, even if it's totally meaningless, that's different. I can do whatever I want. If Strier asks me to do it, there's nobody really to stop me."

"You know, Timothy probably has a badge you could wear. You think that might help?"

"That's a great idea. I'm sure that would be a big help." Timothy had a nice shiny badge pinned to his teddy bear.

"Deputy sheriff. I like that."

It was nice to see her smiling again. I looked up at the clock. "Time to go?"

"You're right; it is." She got up, getting ready to leave. She looked at me with a bemused smile. "So, I'm married to a deputy sheriff, huh? Is that what you're telling me?"

"Yup. That's me."

She picked up her bag and walked to the door. Then, slowly and suggestively, she said, "I'll see ya later, Deputy."

She gave me a big wink and headed out the door.

At least she seemed to be feeling better. I figured reality would come crashing back in soon enough.

7

ater that morning I arrived at Laurel Hill Hospital to speak with Hank Strier. We met in a small office in the anesthesia workroom just off one of the main OR corridors. He was running anesthesia for the entire OR suite.

Periodically stretchers would roll by ferrying patients to and from the holding area, the ORs, and the recovery room. It was like watching a stream of little boats heading out from a harbor onto the high seas to be tossed around at the mercy of the elements, and then returning to safe harbor once the journey was done.

Strier's office barely had room for the small desk he was sitting behind and the single chair in which I sat facing him. Covering most of one wall was a whiteboard showing the OR schedule for the day. There was a box for each OR. Inside each box, written with black marker, were the cases scheduled for that room plus the surgeon and the anesthesia team. I could see that Lucy was supervising two ORs doing orthopedic cases—knees and hips.

It only took a few minutes to get Strier to deputize me, although we didn't call it that. He seemed happy to have my help and understood why I wanted to be able to say I was doing this at his request.

"How about this?" He smiled at me. "I'll tell people you're a national expert on patient safety."

I had to laugh.

That was at best a wild exaggeration. He knew that.

"I have written a couple of papers about patient safety," I said, "but that's about it."

"You give talks too, right?"

"It's pretty much the same talk. I use different examples for different audiences."

"Including talks at national conferences?"

"A few."

"There you go." He pointed at me. "A national expert. Sitting right there." He thought for a moment. "In any case, now that Laurel Hill Hospital is part of the health network, everything that happens here is subject to the recommendations of that committee you sit on. Right?"

"I guess so." I paused. "Of course, that doesn't make me a detective. Patient safety has absolutely nothing to do with solving crimes."

"It makes you the closest thing we've got."

"OK, fine. Let's go with it," I said.

"Focus initially on the anesthesia department and we'll see where it goes from there," he said. He sent me a brief email as I sat there. "I'll tell everyone that we work together a lot at the medical school and that I trust your judgment. Keep it low key. If anyone objects, I'll let you know."

"Thanks," I said. "The fact that Lucy and I are married won't be a problem?"

"Not for me. It's what makes you willing to help. I need to get this place under control, and you are clearly motivated. Have you had any further thoughts?"

"I think we should talk about motive," I said.

"That's the question, isn't it?" he said. "I guess we're assuming that someone deliberately wanted to kill Arnold, and there are certainly a lot of people who really didn't like him at all."

"Not liking him doesn't translate into murder, of course."

"Right. And even then, there are a lot of motives. It could be personal. Someone wanted Arnold dead for something he personally did. Or it could be someone enraged by the takeover process and blaming Arnold for that. But if that's the motive, then half the staff of this hospital are suspects."

"What about the anesthesia department?"

"A lot of people here are very upset. Lucy, Dave Freeman, and I were sent here from Boston Central to start the takeover process. In a few months there are going to be big changes. Everybody knows that."

There was a knock at the door. A woman was standing in the doorway.

"The next case in room seven ate breakfast," she announced.

Strier looked up at the schedule on his wall.

"An ankle?"

"Yes," she said. "It's just local with anesthesia standby. The surgeon seems to be wondering if he could proceed without us."

"Make sure he understands that anesthesia absolutely cannot be involved. If they get halfway through and suddenly decide they need us, we won't be able to do anything at all to help them."

"I told him that. I think they're cancelling." She paused and then continued. "I asked the patient what he had for breakfast. He told me scrambled eggs, bacon, toast, and coffee. I thought he was joking."

"I gather he wasn't."

"He had been told not to eat. He had written instructions not to eat. He's sort of surprised it's such a big deal."

Strier looked over at his board. "Let's assume it's cancelled. See if the next case in room five can be moved in there."

"OK." The woman disappeared.

Strier looked at me and smiled. "This is what I do all day."

"Where were we?" he continued.

"We were talking about motive," I said. "What's going on with the staff here, anyway? Lucy doesn't talk much about it, but I can tell it upsets her. A lot of them seem to be angry. Are they angry about money?"

"Money is definitely a factor," Strier said. "Money and job security. What they have here are twelve anesthesiologists and about fifteen nurse anesthetists. Five of the anesthesiologists are partners. They used to run the place. Now, of course, I do. They each make close to a million dollars a year. Can you imagine that? The other seven anesthesiologists are worker bees. They make much less. They were worked hard and took a lot of call. They basically got dumped on by the partners. Nobody has made partner in years."

"What's happening now that you're here?"

"Now? We're in transition. But the anesthesiologists are an independent corporation and they have a contract. We have to honor that contract until it runs out in a few months. After that, anyone we don't want will have to leave."

"Can most of them stay?"

"If they stay, they'll make an academic salary, three or four hundred thousand. That's a huge hit for the partners, obviously. For the worker bees it's really not a bad deal. We'll treat them much better than the partners did."

"So the partners may leave, but the worker bees may stay?"

"The partners aren't going to stay."

"What about the worker bees? Did they have trouble getting good people?"

"Most of them are OK, but you'd be amazed at some of the stuff going on here." He looked at me for a moment, clearly wondering how much to say. "OK, I'm asking you to help, so I should probably tell you about some of the problems I'm dealing with."

He got up and closed the office door.

"Listen to this. We have one guy who maybe falls asleep when he is giving anesthesia in the middle of the night. Dozes off. Maybe. These are just rumors."

"Uh-oh!" It was hard not to laugh the way Strier was describing it. "That's pretty scary. You say *maybe* falls asleep?"

"Maybe. Probably. Who knows? I'm not going to come here the middle of the night and try to catch him doing it. That would never work. Anyway, I'm moving him to one-day surgery five days a week. He'll only work days from now on."

"But you won't be keeping him?"

"He's a nice guy. He's very competent. If his only problem is dozing off in the middle of the night, we'll just have him work during the day. He's in his sixties."

"He's a worker bee?"

"He's a worker bee. He hasn't been here long. He moved to Boston a few years ago."

"But he's not the only problem?"

"Here's another. We have a young guy who was taking Valium while he was working. To deal with the stress. It was like having a floppy rubber man in the OR. He wasn't fully there. It was very dangerous."

At this point there was another knock. The door opened about a foot and a half and a woman's head appeared. More news for Strier.

"Room twelve is going back on bypass. It will probably be quite a while before they get done. One way or another."

"OK," Strier said. "That room will pretty definitely run late."

The head disappeared and the door closed.

"What was that all about?"

"That's one of our open-heart rooms." He glanced at the schedule. "They're doing a coronary artery procedure. They're having trouble getting the patient off the heart-lung bypass machine. Getting his heart working again."

"What's likely to happen?" I asked.

"They'll try several times. Hopefully they'll succeed. If not—" Strier paused. "Well, eventually they'll stop trying."

"And the patient will die on the operating table? Is that what you mean?"

"Yes." He could tell what I was thinking. "But this is very different from what happened yesterday with Lucy. This patient must have a very bad heart. If he doesn't make it out of the OR, the family will have been fully prepared."

He could see my concern.

"In all likelihood we'll get him off the pump," he said. "We almost always do."

This was not really what I was here to talk about.

"What about the guy taking Valium," I asked. "Is he still here?"

"He was seeing a psychiatrist and the Valium was prescribed."

"So, he was following medical advice."

"Yes. Idiotic medical advice, but medical advice nevertheless. We can't really fault him for it. We took him off the Valium and I talked to his therapist. I did my best to describe why it was completely inappropriate."

"So now he has to deal with his stress some other way."

"Yup."

"Will you keep him?"

"He needs to move on. You want to hear more?"

"Please. This is fascinating."

"Well, one of the biggest problems is sick call. The worker bees get four weeks of vacation each year and ten days of sick call. So guess what?"

"They get sick ten days a year?"

"It's worse than that. They call in sick, but always on a Friday or a Monday."

"Ahh. A long weekend."

"Right. So, I'd come in on a Friday or a Monday, and one or maybe even two of them would have called in sick. It would be seven in the morning with the ORs full of cases ready to start at seven thirty, and I'd suddenly discover that people were not showing up. They wouldn't call in sick until first thing in the morning. It threw everything into chaos."

"And they all do this?"

"No, fortunately just a few. But it was terrible for morale. Lucy really got mad at one of them. Namrata Sharma did it a lot. After the third time, Lucy really laid into her. They were screaming at each other."

"Dave Freeman said something about that yesterday. I really can't imagine Lucy screaming. For any reason."

"She was definitely screaming."

"So, this is another thing people are angry about."

"Definitely. I thought about making them bring in a letter from their doctor, but I don't really think that would work . . . It's like I'm a kindergarten teacher."

"But somehow none of this really sounds like a motive for murder," I said.

"You wouldn't think so, but I have to tell you, some of them take this whole thing very personally. Namrata is very angry at Lucy. In fact, I would have to say Namrata hates Lucy. Needless to say, Namrata will not be staying on."

Strier's phone rang. He picked it up, listened briefly, and hung up.

"I need to go to one of the rooms and see what's going on. Some little interpersonal tempest in a teapot, apparently."

"OK, that's fine. This is a good start. I guess my next step is to talk to some of your staff. Do you have a list?"

He produced one and quickly went down the list identifying partners, worker bees who would be moving on, and anyone he thought might be particularly worth talking to. I made a few notes. I'd be getting Lucy's comments too.

"Thanks," I said. "I'll get back to you."

8

The next evening, Lucy and I were finally alone. I had been up all night working in the ER. I managed to get some sleep during the day, but I was still pretty zoned out. We were sitting out on our little deck doing not very much at all. Decompressing. Basking in the gentle summer breeze. The kids were asleep. Through the various buildings and trees I saw a bit of the Charles River. I could smell the fresh-cut grass along the river banks. When I was a student at MIT, I took long walks along the Charles. I used to sail on it too.

When Lucy and I moved back to Boston, I told her we had to live somewhere near the river. The small house we finally found was a block and a half from the Charles, tucked away behind Peabody Terrace and Mather House. It was a short walk to Harvard Square, and from there it was a pretty straight shot by MBTA to Boston Central Hospital where I worked. And where Lucy normally worked too.

We were lounging in comfortable deck chairs with our feet up on the same soft, cushioned footstool. As I relaxed, letting stress drain out of my body with my eyes closed, Lucy rubbed her feet up against mine. We were both wearing socks—hers had cute little koala bears peering out of a bamboo thicket. It tickled. I reached out for her hand and gave it three little squeezes. This was our secret code for "I love you." She gave me three little squeezes back.

We continued lounging. If we kept this up much longer, I would soon doze off. Lucy finally broke into our silent reverie.

"The police came and talked to me again."

"At the hospital?"

"Yes. One of the detectives had some more questions. But he also had good news."

"How so?"

"They did a fingerprint analysis on all the syringes I drew up for the case. It turns out my fingerprints were on all the syringes except for the syringe labeled vecuronium. That one had no fingerprints on it at all."

She was smiling. I didn't quite get it.

"So, how is that good news?"

"When I drew up the drugs I wasn't wearing gloves, so my fingerprints should have been on all the syringes. But when I actually gave the drugs, I was wearing latex gloves."

I got it.

"So, the police data are consistent with someone substituting that syringe," I said.

"Exactly. They also did an analysis of the drugs in all the syringes I had drawn up for the case. They all contained the correct drug except for the vecuronium syringe. It did contain potassium, but it also contained sulfuric acid and maybe some other stuff too. They've sent it off for a comprehensive analysis."

"It sounds like we were right."

"And there's more. They did the same analysis for all the drug bottles that I drew those syringes up from. They all contained the correct drugs. One of those bottles, which contains 25 cc of vecuronium when you first open it, contained 15 cc of vecuronium when they analyzed it. So that basically says that I did draw up vecuronium. It was a 10 cc syringe."

"All that pretty much confirms that you drew up vecuronium and then someone substituted the syringe. It was not an accident."

She nodded.

"Did you get any idea what the police are thinking?"

"They appear to be convinced that it was a crime. That it was deliberate. But I assume they keep a lot of possibilities open as they investigate. Who knows what they say to each other?"

At this point, she fell silent and we just lay there for a few minutes.

"Oh. I totally forgot. Another thing happened," she said suddenly.

Something about the tone of her voice made me think, *Uh-oh.*

"A reporter from *The Boston World* wants to talk to me. She left a message on my phone. Her name sounds familiar. Gwen Swann. I think you know her."

I did know her.

"I helped her write two articles about medical ethics a year or two ago," I said. "She's very smart. She was a lot of fun to work with."

"I assume I just ignore her?"

"Yes! Definitely ignore her. But I'll call the general counsel's office if that's OK with you." I had talked to them before and knew who to call. "They may want you to refer any questions to them. I think we should get them in the loop."

We had another period of silence. This time I broke it.

"I have an idea."

"Uh-oh. Gideon, you have that gleam in your eye . . . again," she said. She knew about my ideas.

I walked back into the living room and started pacing, trying to organize my thoughts. As she watched me, I could see she was getting alarmed.

"No, Gideon. No. No. No."

"You don't even know what I'm thinking."

"Whatever it is, don't do it." She now stood in the doorway between the porch and the living room.

"It's sort of a weird idea."

"I can tell."

"She's an intelligent woman."

"What? Who?"

"The reporter. Gwen. I think maybe I should talk to her."

"I thought we agreed to ignore her."

"We agreed you should ignore her."

"Then why would you want to talk to her?"

"*Sub rosa,*" I said.

"Sub what?"

"I think maybe I should talk to her *sub rosa.*"

"Gideon, come on. What does *sub rosa* mean? For some reason that makes me think of the OSS during World War II." She had settled herself down on our living room sofa. Perhaps to better watch my performance. She was used to me.

"More like Deep Throat," I said. "You know. Watergate. In a parking garage somewhere at night."

Lucy's expression registered somewhere between alarm and exasperation.

"Gideon, you're starting to scare me."

"I need to think about this."

"Come on, Gideon, time out." Lucy held up her hands in the shape of a T, just like they did during football games.

"I'll think about it," I said.

"Look Gideon, this is your official time-out person telling you to take a time out. Sleep on it. Sit down. Have a cold beer or something."

I continued pacing.

Suddenly she shot me a gleeful look. I could tell she was getting ready to jerk my chain. "This Gwen person, Gideon. What's she like. Young? Attractive? Sexy?"

"Sort of."

"Hah!"

"Look, that has nothing to do with it. She's a reporter. She's also married."

"That sure doesn't guarantee anything these days." Lucy was just teasing. She knew I would never look at another woman.

"She's married to a *woman.*" I wasn't sure what Lucy could do with that.

Not much I guess.

"Gideon, this is getting too weird. Are you telling me you want to meet a newspaper reporter in a parking garage in the middle of the night?"

"I told you, it's called *sub rosa.* It means doing something invisibly. Behind the scenes."

"It's called *nuts.*"

"What's wrong with brilliant? Maybe it's brilliant."

Or maybe both. Couldn't an idea be brilliant and nuts at the same time? Why not?

"Look, Gideon, sleep on it. Don't even think about this tonight."

Lucy went over to her desk and pulled out a bright-orange index card with TIME OUT printed on it in big, bold black letters. She handed it to me with a flourish.

"Now it's official. See what it says? TIME OUT."

"OK, OK, OK." I held up the card and looked at it. This was new. "Where did you get this idea?"

"The World Cup. I made up yellow ones, orange ones, and red ones."

"Let me see."

Lucy went over to her desk and came back with a little stack of brightly colored TIME OUT cards.

"What do I need to do to get a red one?" I asked.

"I don't know. But I'm sure we'll find out soon enough."

I went to her and gave her a kiss.

"This is good. I like this. Thank you for doing this for me."

She laughed and gave me a little punch on my upper arm. A pretty hard little punch, actually. "Yeah, right. Now you're just trying to butter me up. Again."

"No. Not at all," I said, but I realized of course she was right. "Well, maybe just a bit. But I do think it's a great idea." I really did.

"Stick the card in your wallet so you'll see it every time you open it up."

"I obey," I said, doing what she asked.

"Obey the card, too."

"We'll see."

She punched me again, maybe a little harder.

We'll see. This time I just thought it silently.

Sub rosa.

9

The next day was my favorite day of the entire year. It was blood-drawing day for all the first-year medical students, over one hundred of them. Today they learned how to draw blood, with me as their teacher.

Lucy kept telling me to stop volunteering for stuff like that. And, of course, she was right. I needed to learn to say no. In fact, we practiced it. She would ask me to do something ridiculous, and I was supposed to say no. If I did, she rewarded me with a kiss. "Good boy." Then she would ask me to do a bunch of other stupid things and I was supposed to say no to all of them. Or else I could say, "Let me check my schedule and I'll call you back." That was as good as saying no. It gave me time to think.

My problem was that I tended to say yes, and then I was stuck. And once people knew you said yes, you were always the first person they thought of when they needed something.

But I was not about to give up blood-drawing day. It was too much fun.

The entire class trooped into a large conference room right next to the main Boston Central emergency room. Each student got a syringe from a big box of syringes I had brought along. I had the students pair up, and I chose a partner for myself. My partner and I would demonstrate how it was done. Then the rest of the students would draw blood from each other.

I chose a student who had done research with laboratory animals for several years and had drawn blood from them many times. She had no problem drawing blood from the large, bulging vein on the inside of my elbow. I described what she was doing to the class. Most of the students watched carefully. The ones who couldn't get close enough watched on video monitors.

Then it was my turn. I pretended to be a totally inept novice who was very nervous about everything. I had not prepared my partner for this. She was laughing at my obvious act, but at the same time she looked slightly alarmed as my bumbling persona approached her arm with the syringe. I prepped the vein in her elbow, putting on a tourniquet and rubbing her skin with an alcohol swab, all the time doing my best to portray extreme timidity. But her vein was also big and bulging, so despite my apparent anxiety and trepidation, I was somehow able to gently stick the needle in and draw a syringe full of blood with no problem. She helped by holding her skin down and telling me what angle to use, along with a variety of other advice. This, of course, was really for the students—not for me.

The rest of the class started in on each other. Most of them were able to do it on the first try, but some were not as fortunate. Their partners wound up being Voodoo dolls, subjected to multiple needle sticks and multiple bruises from unsuccessful attempts. But everyone eventually succeeded, and most of them clearly enjoyed the experience. For them it was one more milestone along the road to becoming physicians.

As we were winding up, one of my fellow ER doctors came into the room.

"Hey, Gideon, you need to look at your email."

"What for?"

"There is a message you need to read. It came in a couple of minutes ago. We all got it. It claims to be from Dr. Jones, the chief of surgery at Laurel Hill Hospital. But it's clearly not from him. It's some kind of spoofed email."

I finished up with the students and found a PC in the ER that was not being used. I opened my email and there it was.

The subject line said, *He sure had it coming.* I read on.

Well, I guess you have all heard that the CEO of our health system is dead, and the rumors are flying. Was he deliberately murdered? And if so, who did it?

Let's face it. It's not as if there aren't a whole lot of people who hated him. Like almost everyone employed by Laurel Hill Community Hospital, for example. If we are not all being forced out by the merger, we are all having to take massive pay cuts. I am sure there must be some way to merge a hospital into a health system with some dignity. But James Arnold sure didn't care about dignity. He managed to do it in the most degrading and humiliating way possible.

But then, who says it was murder? What happened to plain old malpractice? You may have noticed that our anesthesia department is being taken over by a bunch of pointy-headed academics. They may think they know how to do research, but who says they know the first thing about patient care?

Dr. Rivera may be a wannabee researcher, but she sure is a walking disaster area in the operating room. See the attached M&M sheet for examples of her work. See if you can guess which cases she was involved in.

But if you ask me, the real reason that asshole got killed was that he couldn't keep his dick in his pants. Just go look in the men's OR locker room in the fourth toilet stall and you'll see what I mean. He used to tell his residents that you weren't a real doctor until you had your first nurse. If it was female and it moved, he would try to stick his prick in it. Look for a husband married to a nurse.

I'll keep you all informed as this develops further.

Joseph Jones, MD
Chief, Department of Surgery
Laurel Hill Community Hospital

This email even had Jones's signature scrawled above his name, which of course didn't mean a thing. It was easy to cut and paste a signature.

Obviously, Jones did not send this incredibly unprofessional email unless he had suddenly lost all his marbles. Either someone hacked his email account or spoofed the sending address. It appeared to be addressed to a mailing list of all the clinical staff of the entire health system, not just Laurel Hill Hospital. Plus, a number of names that were clearly local media, newspapers and TV stations. There were also email addresses that looked like they belonged to law firms. I thought I recognized a couple that had dealt with high-profile malpractice cases in the past.

"Dr. Rivera" was Lucy. Luciana Rivera. The email essentially accused her of being incompetent. I opened the attachment. It had the scanned handout from a recent anesthesiology M&M (morbidity and mortality) conference. The handout briefly described three cases where there had been problems or which illustrated interesting clinical issues.

There were no patient names on the cases and no doctor names, either. I had no idea which cases might have been Lucy's, if any.

As I sat there reading that email, a second message appeared from Dr. Jones. This one stated 1) that the previous email was not sent by him, 2) that he had no idea who sent it, and 3) that his email account was being shut down.

I printed out the first email and headed over to Laurel Hill Hospital to show it to Lucy. If at all possible, I wanted to be there when she found out about it.

When I arrived, I went straight to the OR locker room and changed into scrubs. It was a large room with over a hundred lockers, connected to a smaller washroom which had sinks, urinals, and five toilet stalls. Two security guards wearing green uniforms and hospital insignia were already in the washroom, standing watch over the toilets. Presumably in response to the fake Jones email.

I showed my ID.

"I'm Gideon Lowell. I am working with the anesthesia department. I'm helping them figure out what's going on. There's apparently something about one of the toilet stalls?"

"It's right down there," one of them told me, pointing to the fourth stall, now suddenly famous.

I opened the door and looked in. There on the off-white metal divider wall was a four-foot picture drawn with black marker. Two naked figures were having sex. The male was drawn a few inches above the female, so you could see his erect penis spurting fluid. He was wearing only a surgeon's cap and was reasonably identifiable as James Arnold. To dispel any possible confusion, however, the initials *J A* had been written close to his head.

I did not recognize the female beneath him with her legs spread. But the initials said *A L*. She appeared to be panting, perhaps because the word *PANT* was written three times in capital letters just above her head.

It was a pretty good picture. The artist definitely had talent.

Stepping back out of the stall, I turned to the two security men.

"Do you know how long this has been here?"

"At least a few weeks, but probably much longer," one of them replied. "A lot of people knew about it."

"But nobody did anything?"

"I don't think anyone reported it."

I guessed that people got used to seeing graffiti on bathroom walls and just tuned it out.

"I assume that anyone who saw this was a male? Right? Since this is the men's locker room," I asked. "Female nurses would presumably have known nothing about this?"

"Not until today," the guard laughed. "A bunch of nurses came in and looked at it a few minutes ago. They had us come in first and make sure nobody was here."

"What about the woman in the picture? Do we know who A. L. is? Are those the initials of a nurse?"

Or maybe a female doctor.

"Yes, it's a nurse. Allison Lange. And she apparently had no idea this was here. She came in here ten minutes ago and looked at it."

"Oh my God. Any reaction?"

"None. She just looked. It was probably just a few seconds but seemed longer. Then she just walked out without saying a thing. Her face was like stone."

I can't imagine what she must have been thinking. Probably not much. She was probably stunned.

It sounded to me like this was just random graffiti. Whoever sent Jones's email must have known about it and decided to mention it in the message.

"You know it was her?" I asked.

"The picture looks a lot like her." He was nodding and clearly trying not to laugh. "The initials match. Yeah, it was her."

"Is she married?"

"I have no idea. People take off their rings when they scrub for the OR. You can't tell anything by looking for rings."

"Do you know anything about them having an affair?'

"I have no idea." The security guard waved his hands as if to say he wanted nothing to do with that question. "And you'd better believe I wasn't about to ask."

The second guard added, "Apparently he did it a lot though. A lot of affairs. The nurses were just now telling us that, but we knew about it anyway. He was notorious." The other guard nodded.

"Wow," I said. "What do you think will happen with the picture?" It occurred to me the police might not want it erased.

"We'll do whatever the police tell us to do. They should be here soon. Maybe they'll take the metal wall somewhere and store it. They could easily undo the bolts that are holding it in place."

"You mean maybe they'll take the wall to the police evidence room? Like on TV?"

"I have no idea. Maybe they'll just take a picture of it."

I walked out of the locker room area into the main OR corridor and made my way to Strier's office in the anesthesia work room. I had called ahead.

"I just read the email," he said. "My God. What's going on?"

"Where's Lucy?" I wanted to talk to Lucy as soon as possible. That was my biggest concern.

"She doesn't know anything about this. I wanted to let you tell her. She's in an OR doing a case by herself. I'll have someone take over her room, and I'll take her off the schedule for the rest of the day."

"What about the M&M sheets?"

He threw up his hands. "Oh great! I hadn't focused on that at all. I need to figure out how those got outside our department. This whole thing is getting much too strange."

I tried to imagine how Lucy was going to react. I wanted to

go and put my arms around her, hold her very tight, and tell her everything was OK.

Of course, everything was not OK.

We walked down the hall to Lucy's OR. A nurse anesthetist came with us. I stood outside while Strier and the nurse went in. A minute later, Strier emerged with Lucy in tow. She was clearly surprised to see me there.

"We need to talk," I said.

10

Lucy was pretty resilient about the email. Her basic attitude was that she was respected by everybody she respected, so who cared what some random idiot was saying. Especially if he (or she) was saying it anonymously. We decided the best thing was for me to press ahead and do my best to figure out what was going on. Every week I worked roughly three eight-hour shifts in the ER. I'd continue to do that, but the rest of the time I'd focus on trying to figure this out.

The next day I was back in Strier's little office at Laurel Hill Hospital and it was suddenly very busy. It felt like I was in an air traffic control tower with no windows. All I could see was the OR schedule written on Strier's whiteboard on the wall.

Every few minutes Strier's phone would ring or someone would stop by his office door, and suddenly there would be some new problem he had to solve. A room was running late. A case had been cancelled. A surgeon was tied up operating at a different hospital and was going to be late, and it was anybody's guess when he might actually arrive. A constant stream of near misses and redirection. But no mid-air collisions—nothing like the CEO of your health system having cardiac arrest and dying in one of your operating rooms.

None of those today.

Not yet anyway.

I sat there thinking it would drive me crazy if I had to deal with little stuff like this all day long. But Strier took it all in stride.

I had come over because I needed more information and I wanted somebody to talk to. I had drawn myself a little map of Laurel Hill's fourteen ORs. It showed the connecting scrub rooms between each pair of ORs. It showed the several corridors that connected the ORs to the pre-op holding area, to the recovery room, and also directly to the CTICU where all the heart patients went after surgery. Post-op heart patients stayed right next to the ORs in case they had to be rolled back in for emergencies like when hearts suddenly started to leak blood through the suture lines.

I also added the locker rooms, the break rooms, and anything else I could remember. Before coming to see Strier I walked around the entire OR suite once again. In the process I discovered several additional rooms—some for storing equipment, others for mysterious purposes that I couldn't figure out. There was also a back door from one of the rear OR corridors to a staircase. This door appeared to be unlocked but had a big sign on it saying an alarm would sound if opened. I started adding all this to my map but finally wound up using two full pages to make up a totally new map that was much more accurate and complete.

When I showed this to Strier, I had to push his PC way over to one side of his little desk and spread out the map.

He examined it for a moment. "Pretty good. What's it for?"

"I'm doing this because I'm trying to imagine exactly how somebody might have gone about switching the vecuronium syringe in Lucy's OR. The more I think about it, the more complicated it all seems."

"How do you mean, complicated?" Strier asked. "What's so complicated about switching one syringe for another?"

"Well, I started trying to imagine how I would go about doing that myself. For example, I would have to do it without attracting attention. At the beginning of the day, there must be all sorts of people scurrying around all over the place. I would need to blend in. I would also need to figure out when Lucy's OR was empty, and it's not like there's a closet or someplace where I could hide and peek out through a crack to see when the coast was clear. And I wouldn't be able to just stand there in the hallway looking into the room. That wouldn't work. Right?"

"Right. If you did that, you'd stand out like a sore thumb."

"So, unless I was working right in Lucy's OR or in the OR immediately next door on the other side of the scrub room, there would be no way of knowing when Lucy's room was empty without walking past it, which I might have to do several times before I finally found it empty."

Strier nodded.

"So, maybe I could somehow just stand down the hall and wait until I saw Lucy leaving to go meet Arnold in the holding area. But I don't really think there is any place for me to stand around and wait without calling attention to myself."

"People would definitely notice," Strier said.

"Do you think it would look suspicious if I walked around the OR corridors wearing a mask?"

"Not if you were in a corridor right outside an OR," Strier said. "I doubt anyone would notice that."

"OK then, let's assume I have to walk past Lucy's OR several times before I finally find it empty. Where could I go in between these times where people wouldn't notice me?"

"I'm not sure. Pretty much anywhere you went to sit or stand around, people would start to wonder what you were doing. And you would definitely stand out if you were doing that and continuing to wear your mask."

I thought some more. Then I suddenly had a funny idea.

"How about this?" I said. "Suppose I go and sit in one of the locker room toilet stalls. Then every couple of minutes, I flush the toilet, walk out into the OR area, go past Lucy's OR, and then return to the toilet stall if her OR is not empty. And I just keep doing that and hope for the best. If the OR is ever empty, it would only take a few seconds to switch the syringe."

"Of course, you might never succeed," Strier said.

I shrugged.

"But you're right," he said. "That would probably work. Anyone coming into the locker room would just be there for a minute or two changing into scrubs, and then they'd go on out to the ORs. There would be no one to notice that you were constantly going back and forth."

By this time, Strier was looking at me with considerable amusement.

I doubted if Sherlock Holmes ever had this kind of discussion with Dr. Watson. As I recall, Holmes could just look at a few seemingly random details and then suddenly figure it all out. That was clearly not my style.

In fact, I would likely never know if the perpetrator (I was now mentally calling this person *the perpetrator*) actually used a toilet stall as a place to hide out between forays into the OR corridors. To tell the truth, I didn't seem to be getting very far in figuring out what had happened.

As I came to this realization, Lucy appeared in the anesthesia workroom and Strier waved her in to join us.

Strier had tried to take Lucy off the schedule, but she refused, saying it would look bad. She thought the best thing to do was to just keep working as if nothing had happened.

"What's up? Taking a break?" I stood to give her my chair and sat on the corner of Strier's small desk.

"I'm in between cases in both my rooms," she said. "I have two nurse anesthetists and they're both setting up for the next case. What are you two talking about? Me?"

"No," I said, "not at all. I'm bouncing ideas off Strier. Trying to figure out exactly what happened."

"Gideon has some really off-the-wall ideas," Strier said, laughing.

"I'm used to it," she said. "That's what Gideon does."

Then she turned and looked at me.

"So, are you making progress?" From my expression I think she could sense the answer was no. "I hope? Maybe?" she said.

"No. Not really. Sorry, but at least I am trying to define a few of the questions to ask. Like how exactly would you go about switching a syringe in an OR for the first case of the day. What do you think? What would you do?"

Lucy thought about it for a moment. "Well, I'd have to walk around the OR area like I was just doing my job. And hope nobody noticed me. Actually, one of the detectives was asking me about that."

"About what?"

"About whether I had seen anybody walking around the OR area who didn't seem to belong there."

"Had you?"

Lucy looked at me with a funny expression.

"I told him I did sort of remember seeing someone walking past my OR. This was from about halfway down the corridor when I was heading toward the holding area to wait for Arnold to arrive. I remember wondering what she was doing."

"You never told me about that."

"Yeah. So much has happened. This was one tiny part of a long interview with the detective. And I didn't get a good look at her anyway. It was probably nothing."

"It was a her?"

"Actually, it looked sort of like Namrata. But I couldn't really tell. And I wasn't paying any attention at all."

"But you told the detective about it?"

"Yes."

"And you told him it looked like Namrata?"

"I told him that it looked sort of like her. Thin. Female. The way she held herself reminded me of Namrata. Whatever. I don't know. It made me think of Namrata."

At that point, Strier and I looked directly at each other. I'm not sure exactly what we were thinking. Probably some combination of "Oh my God" and "Uh-oh." And then, Strier's office door suddenly jerked open. There stood a very angry Namrata.

She was indeed thin, although not skinny. About five feet nine. Early thirties. Clearly Indian. Jet-black hair, mostly covered by a light-blue paper surgical cap. Quite striking. Overall a very attractive woman, even when enraged.

"Bitch! You total bitch!" Namrata screamed, glaring at Lucy.

Everybody in the workroom turned to look.

"You total slimeball!" Namrata continued.

Lucy just sat there stunned. I was too. This was way beyond the pale.

"You told the police I switched that syringe, didn't you! Didn't you!"

Lucy stared at her, speechless.

"They're interviewing everybody," Namrata said. "They are

asking everybody about me. Where I was. Who I was with."
Namrata glared at Strier and me, and then fixed back on Lucy.
"I was nowhere near your fucking OR. I was downstairs in one-
day surgery. Everybody knows that. Everybody saw me there
the whole time. You are going to fucking regret this, you bitch."

Strier stood behind his little desk.

"Namrata," he said calmly. "Please sit down."

He was talking very softly but sternly, as if addressing a
child. At the same time, he gestured Lucy and me out of the
room with one of his hands.

Namrata sat, looking flustered.

As Lucy and I left, Strier closed his office door. We walked
silently past the gawking audience. Once we got out into the
corridor, Lucy finally spoke.

"She's the bitch."

11

After the big blowup with Namrata, Lucy had to get back to running her two ORs, and we didn't get a chance to talk again until that evening. But even then we didn't have time to talk much. I helped her get the kids ready for bed. Then I told her I had to go to the library for a couple of hours. We had decided that the public library would be a good place to do Google searches anonymously so I wouldn't leave footprints on my home PC. Or little footprints out there on the internet pointing to my home PC.

But I didn't go to the library.

About thirty minutes later, I pulled into a large concrete parking garage that was attached to a suburban shopping mall west of Boston. It was around nine thirty in the evening in the middle of the week. I was on the ground floor. There was room for maybe a couple hundred cars, but it was at most one quarter full. Aside from the buzz of very distant traffic, there were no sounds at all.

Gwen Swann, the *Boston World* reporter, had agreed to meet me. I told her roughly where I would park, and I was supposed to look for a light-blue Honda sedan. After a few minutes, a light-blue Honda sedan appeared. It flashed its high beams once and glided into a parking slot about twenty yards from mine. I felt like I was in a movie. I was now *sub rosa* for sure—not even Lucy knew I was doing this. It would be simpler if she didn't know.

I walked over and knocked twice on the passenger's window. The door unlocked and I got in. I wondered if this was how Bob Woodward and Deep Throat had done it.

Gwen smiled at me from the driver's seat. She was in her mid-thirties, thin, and had short, light-brown hair. Some males can describe women's hairstyles. Not me. Women's shoes are also a mystery. Makeup—another total mystery. But I digress.

Gwen's clothes looked casual but fairly stylish. I wasn't sure what a soccer mom really looked like, but that's what popped into my head as I looked at her.

"Hi," I said. I wasn't sure exactly what to say next. This was new territory for me. A *sub rosa* meeting with the media.

"You're OK with this?" I asked. "Meeting like this?"

"Yes. Absolutely. This is totally fine."

"You do it all the time?"

"Not all the time. Sometimes."

Sitting on a little shelf between the two front seats of her car were a small tape recorder and a pad of paper with a mechanical pencil clipped to it. Looking at them brought home the reality of what I was about to do.

"Is that thing on?" I asked, gesturing at the tape recorder. Actually, tape was probably obsolete these days. What did you call a tape recorder that didn't actually use tape?

"No, it's off," she said, "and don't worry. I won't turn it on without asking your permission."

"Thanks." I did my best to smile back at her. "Where to start?" That came out with a nervous little laugh.

"Just start anywhere. Just talk for a while. I'll start asking you questions when it feels right."

"OK, but first of all, how does this all work? I mean, if I tell you something, what do you do with it?"

"Anything you tell me here is confidential if you want it to be. Is that what you mean? Don't worry about that." She smiled. "I'm like a priest."

"A priest. Good. But how does it work?"

"It's up to you. If you want to be anonymous, then I might quote you but never mention your name. I'd identify you as a member of the medical staff or something like that. But you can also tell me things totally off the record. Background. It can be very helpful for me if you are willing to do that. I don't print anything you say unless I get confirmation from other sources."

She paused for a moment and then continued. "You define what confidential means, Gideon. It's whatever you want."

"Can anyone make you tell them that I'm talking to you?"

"The only person I might tell is my editor. Other than that I would go to jail to protect your anonymity if I had to. But it won't come to that. Don't worry."

I took a deep breath. "I called you because I enjoyed working with you last year. When you wrote those articles on medical ethics. Those articles were really good."

She laughed. "Of course we never met secretly in a parking garage. As I recall, I always came to your office."

I grinned.

"Gideon, I am naturally intrigued by your suggestion that we meet here."

"Yeah. And thanks for coming here, by the way. This may turn out to be a totally stupid idea on my part. But I am hoping we can help each other."

"I assume this must have something to do with all the recent events at Laurel Hill Hospital. Events that involved your wife."

"However did you guess?"

We watched as a black SUV pulled into the slot next to us. In all the movies I'd seen, the CIA drove around in black SUVs. It stopped and nothing happened for a while. I watched it sit there out of the corner of my eye and had trouble focusing on what I was saying. Finally, a woman with two children got out and headed into the mall.

"I definitely want this to be anonymous," I said. "I don't want anyone to know that I'm talking to you, or even suspect that I might be. What I am really interested in is helping you get the record straight. Does that make sense?"

"Yes, that certainly makes sense."

"In my experience the media often tends to get things all balled up. I want to try to keep the media focused on what's really going on, if that's at all possible. With your help, of course. So it doesn't go totally batshit, running off in ridiculous directions.

And I don't want Lucy dragged through the mud. I thought that if I told you everything I know, then you could help *The Boston World* write about it more intelligently and more accurately. Instead of printing wild speculation just because nobody tells you what's really happening."

"I can do that." She gave me a big, funny smile. I suddenly wondered whether maybe I was the proverbial canary about to be swallowed by a cat. Clearly reporters had their own agendas. But as long as everything was anonymous, I thought this would be OK. I just had to make sure that nobody at work knew I was talking like this to the media.

"And I also think you might be able to help me," I continued, "if only by telling me things you hear. You'll be hearing a lot of things I don't hear about."

"That's fine. If I get good information from you, I'm happy to reciprocate. The more you know, the more help you can be to me. That's a fact."

We spent about an hour talking about everything that was going on. She asked me a whole lot of questions, and I answered as best as I could. Questions like exactly what happened in the operating room. What was vecuronium? What was potassium? What did they do? How was the takeover affecting everybody at Laurel Hill Hospital? A whole bunch of questions about Lucy. She jotted things down on the notepad. I had asked her not to use the tape recorder.

I also asked her what she knew. There wasn't much that I didn't already know. But that was fine. She'd probably hear a lot more in the days to come.

Finally, we talked about tradecraft. At least, that was what they called it on TV and in the movies. I had decided that if I was going *sub rosa*, I needed tradecraft. If nothing else, it would be fun. I decided that I did not need a trench coat or a hat with a brim that could be bent down over my eyes. That stuff was all at least sixty years out of date if it ever existed at all.

First of all, I had bought a so-called throwaway cell phone. I showed it to Gwen.

"I'll use this to call you, but only from somewhere outside the hospital and nowhere near my home. Other than that, I am going to keep the battery out of the phone, and the SIM card out too."

I showed her the little baggie I had to store the SIM card in.

"This is probably overkill," I said, "but you never know. I'm pretty sure they put things into cell phones that they don't want anybody to know about. Things they can switch on to track terrorists. Things that record everywhere you ever go, all the time, even when you think the phone is off."

I would err on the side of overkill. Gwen looked amused.

If she wanted to talk to me, she could send me an email from a throwaway email account. I gave her a printout of a random phishing email I had recently received. Something to the effect that my email account would be discontinued if I didn't reply immediately with my login and password.

"Please send me this exact message if you want to talk, but not urgently. If it is urgent, add a second period to the end of the first sentence. If you do that, I'll drop everything and call you back as soon as I can." She folded the message up and tucked it into her notepad.

"This is fun," she said, giggling. "Most people don't do this."

"Most people?"

"I take that back. Nobody. Nobody else does this."

At the end of all this, we shook hands.

"One more question before you go, Gideon." Gwen put her hand briefly on my arm to stop me from getting out of the car. "I somehow have the idea that one of your ancestors was a pirate, and that you're named after him. I think you once told me something like that. Is that right?"

"Yes, that's correct," I said. "Captain Gideon Lowell. He was commissioned as a privateer in the French and Indian Wars. I am indeed named after him. My father had a strange sense of humor."

My father had been a historian specializing in Colonial America. He had passed away several years ago, shortly after my thirty-fifth birthday. I still don't know why he named me after a pirate. But it grew on you. I was actually rather proud of it.

"So, how did being a privateer make him a pirate?"

"Well, family lore seems to suggest that once he got out on the high seas, he got carried away and started preying on neutral shipping. Not just enemy ships."

"And that makes him a pirate?"

"Or something like that. Of course, he didn't live on a pirate island in the Caribbean. He lived in Amesbury, Massachusetts. He was a pretty tame, civilized pirate."

"Well, Gideon," she smiled, "I hope you know what this means. It means that you have official pirate genes."

"I guess I do." I hadn't thought of it that way. Maybe Captain Gideon had ADD too.

"And I think you've inherited some of his finer pirate qualities."

"Thanks a lot. They should come in handy."

"I think they will."

12

"Roberta wants to talk to you. I'm afraid she has bad news," Strier said.

I had stopped by his office at Laurel Hill Hospital to touch base. "Should I call her office and make an appointment?"

"She's here now. Freeman's giving her a tour. She wanted to see this place again in person."

Roberta Patel was chair of the anesthesia department at Boston Central Hospital and one of the national leaders in the field. She was Strier's boss. Lucy's too.

"The scene of the crime," I said.

"Exactly. The scene of the crime. She wanted to get her mind around what happened. She'll be back here shortly."

A few minutes later Roberta appeared.

"Gideon," she greeted me with a big smile. "How lucky. We can all talk."

I extended my hand and received her signature handshake, very firm.

Roberta was a real character. Around fifty, very thin, medium height, with prematurely gray, curly frizzy hair that seemed to resist any attempt to tame it. To put it mildly, Roberta could sometimes be a little intense. I remembered once watching her argue with a six-foot-five-inch orthopedic surgeon. It was really funny. I got the feeling he was afraid she might bite.

But she was very smart and fair. And very decisive. Whenever she got hold of a problem, she wouldn't let go until she solved it. I had learned all that from Lucy.

"We need to talk about your wife," she said. "The network wants me to take Lucy off patient care."

I had been afraid something like this might happen. There were a lot of rumors spewing out from the executive offices of the Boston Central Health System. It was as if someone had tossed a cherry bomb into a hive full of wasps, and now the wasps were all out buzzing around, furious. No big surprise. Their CEO had been murdered, after all, an apparent inside job at one of their own hospitals.

"Can you just bring Lucy back to Boston Central Hospital?" I asked.

"No, they're talking about the network as a whole."

"That really doesn't make any sense. She did her best to keep Arnold alive."

"They don't care. And it's not worth arguing with them. Not now. They're too steamed up."

"They're a bunch of idiots."

"They're saying maybe she should have recognized that it wasn't her syringe," Roberta said. "If she had done that, none of this would have happened."

"Seriously? She should have noticed that the label was in a slightly different location?"

"That's what they're saying."

"That was a tiny difference. It was barely noticeable even when you knew what to look for. And it was Lucy who figured out what had happened, for crying out loud. If she hadn't stopped people from cleaning up that room, we wouldn't have the vaguest idea."

"They don't care," Roberta repeated, "and I'm afraid I have to do something. Unfortunately, they control all my budgets, so I can't just tell them to fuck off. That's of course what I'd really love to do, but I can't." Roberta gave us a tiny little smile.

Money was a constant source of conflict between the network administration and the clinical departments. We all knew that.

"Lucy's not going to be happy," I said.

"I'll take her off the OR schedule for a while. She can do

other things. Outpatient pre-ops. Anesthesia consults. Things like that."

"What about night call and weekend call?" Strier asked.

Roberta thought for a minute.

"Let's leave her there for now. We can take this one step at a time. Good point."

"For how long?" I asked.

"We'll have to see. The network's creating a special committee to look into this. But listen to this. The police told them they're not allowed to investigate, so the committee is going to *assess policy*."

"Assess policy? What the heck does that mean?" I asked.

"Basically, it means they are going to run around investigating, but they're going to call it something else. Officially they'll be looking to see if they need to make any policy changes."

"Like maybe to make sure another health network CEO doesn't get bumped off at Laurel Hill Hospital any time soon?" I suggested.

"Gideon, that's not funny." Roberta laughed. She paused for a moment. "Basically, it means we should just lay low for a while and wait for the dust to settle. We don't do anything that might rile them up."

I thought for a moment. "I assume it would be a big help if someone figured out what actually happened."

"Yes, if someone did that, I think we could put this whole thing behind us and move on. And I do appreciate your offer to help, but you have to be careful. You have my blessing to talk to anyone in our department. But I am not sure it would be good to talk to a lot of people outside our department. Unless we already know them pretty well."

I wasn't sure exactly where that left me.

"Who is going to tell all this to Lucy?" I asked.

"I just saw her," Roberta said. "She's in one of the ORs right now. I'll go talk to her. Maybe there's something else she'd actually like to do. This could be an opportunity for Lucy to do something interesting while we wait for it all to blow over. I'll tell her that."

"I don't think Lucy will see it that way."

"I'll do my best to sugarcoat the pill."

I doubted that would help.

* * *

I found out for sure later that evening.

"I don't want to talk about it."

Those were the first words out of Lucy's mouth when she walked in the door. She got home about half an hour after I did.

I wasn't sure what to do or say. But I had to try.

"Listen, focus on the positive. Do you love your kids? Do you love your family?"

She sort of glared at me.

"Yes, I do."

"Should the health network go fuck itself?"

She continued to glare.

"Yes, it should."

"Good. Enough said. Let's cook dinner."

So we started doing that.

13

To help me get a better feeling for the Laurel Hill anesthesia department, Strier invited me to one of their biweekly M&M conferences, which was supposed to be a learning experience for the medical staff. The goal was to improve patient care. Strier, Freeman, and Lucy took turns leading it, and today was her turn.

Strier suggested that I show up about fifteen minutes late, in part so I could slip in unnoticed and in part because he thought the second case would be particularly "instructive." Not because of the case itself, but because of the anesthesiologist who would be presenting it. I had no idea what to expect.

Lucy was sitting up on a slightly raised dais at the front of the room, which was half full with about twenty people distributed around in small groups. These were the Laurel Hill anesthesiologists and nurse anesthetists who were not still doing cases. It was four fifteen and most of the ORs had finished for the day.

I picked up a handout from a little table just inside the door. It was a single page with a brief description of three cases. Jones's spoofed email had contained an M&M sheet just like this, and had suggested that one or more of those cases illustrated some kind of incompetence on Lucy's part. Apparently, my wife hadn't been involved in any of those cases. *Weird.* But then the whole email thing was very weird.

The discussion of the first case was winding down. The second case was titled *Difficult Intubation* on the handout. Alan Mason stood up to present the case, periodically glancing down at a sheet of paper.

"The patient was a forty-six-year-old man who came for elective shoulder surgery. He was otherwise healthy. His physical exam was unremarkable except for the fact that he was five feet nine inches tall, two hundred and thirty pounds, and very muscular. His airway did not appear to be unusual, although he did have an eighteen-inch, muscular neck and a two-finger-breadth distance between his chin and his Adam's apple."

At this point Lucy interrupted. "Did you obtain those measurements prior to the case, or are those numbers you got later?"

Alan stared straight ahead for a second or two; then he glared at Lucy. "As you very well know, I got those measurements after surgery. You made me go to his room to get them."

Lucy looked taken aback. I wasn't sure why she had asked that question. I wondered if consciously or subconsciously she was trying to provoke a reaction. If so, she had succeeded.

He continued to glare. "The only reason I had to get those numbers was that you put this case on the M&M schedule. What's your point in asking that question? Why don't you just spit it out?" Alan was starting to lose it. This was clearly one of the things Strier wanted me to see.

"Alan, let's just proceed. Why don't you tell us what happened next," Lucy said.

Alan stood there for a moment not saying anything, but then looked down at his notes and continued.

"I induced anesthesia with propofol and gave vecuronium. Then when I went to intubate I was unable to see his chords. I tried to pass the tube in blindly but was unsuccessful. I tried several times. I also tried with a smaller diameter tube, with and without a stylette. I tried a Miller laryngoscope. Nothing worked."

"What finally happened?" Lucy asked.

"Well, I think I tried for about fifteen minutes, and then Strier appeared. Someone must have called him. He asked if he could try. So I let him."

Alan was clearly angry again. "Strier tried several times and finally got the tube in. By that time he was using a number six tube and a Miller scope."

"So what can we learn from this?" Lucy asked, now clearly trying to be low key. This time she was asking the room.

But Alan finally lost it.

"Look, I get it that I don't have any future here. I get it that I'm going to have to sell my house and look for another job. But I don't need this shit."

Alan glared at Lucy.

"So, I had trouble getting the tube in," he continued angrily. "Big deal. Who are you to sit in judgment on me? Huh? What about you? You bump people off in your OR. And on top of that you leave your clothes in your lover's bed. What about that?"

This was way beyond the pale. I wanted to walk up to him, smile, knock his teeth down his throat without any warning, and then politely inquire, "Does that answer your question?"

Lucy must have been prepared for the possibility of some reaction, but she couldn't have been expecting anything like this. She glared back at him. "Alan, you are out of line."

I couldn't just sit there quietly and let my wife take garbage like this, but I wasn't sure what to do. Fortunately, Strier walked up to the dais, clearly angry. When he got there, he turned. "That's enough," he looked around the room and then added, "I will be helping Lucy run the remainder of this conference."

He looked directly at Alan Mason and said in a very cold voice, "Sit down."

Mason obeyed, now glowering at Strier.

Strier addressed the whole room. "First of all, I want to say that I fully appreciate that this is a stressful time for all of us. Major changes are going on and there's nothing we can do about that. Change is coming."

He held up a finger as if chastising a child. "But that is absolutely no excuse for unprofessional behavior. I cannot overemphasize this." He paused and looked around the room. "Unprofessional behavior is not in your self-interest. Wherever you go in the years to come, people will write us and call us to ask about you. When you apply for jobs, they will contact us.

When you apply for medical licenses, they will contact us. And we will provide fair and honest comments. We want to help you put your best foot forward."

He paused again. The room was very quiet, everyone transfixed.

"We want you to succeed," he said.

He stepped down from the dais and walked out into the audience.

"I also assure you that if you act in an unacceptable and unprofessional fashion here, that fact will be passed on as part of our comments. And believe me, you do not want that to happen."

He paused again. "Any questions?"

There were none.

"Please think very seriously about what I just said."

Then Strier looked at Alan. "Alan, please stay after this conference. I want to speak with you."

Strier pulled another chair up onto the dais and sat down next to Lucy, gesturing for her to continue. She looked a bit shell-shocked but recovered quickly as she spoke.

"Well, Hank, since we have you up here, maybe you can give us your perspective on the case. You finally got the tube in. Did you do anything special?"

"You know"—Strier shook his head—"I really don't think I did. Every few months I get called into an OR for this exact problem. And whenever that happens, I have a huge advantage. I am totally fresh, and I know ahead of time that it's going to be difficult. I'm not caught by surprise. I honestly think that is why I often succeed. I don't have any special tricks."

Lucy then started a general discussion of how to assess an airway if you anticipated a potentially difficult intubation. Finally, she went on to the third case. Everything went very smoothly.

No big surprise. By five o'clock, the conference ended.

Lucy came up to me. "Well, now you see firsthand what this place is like."

I shook my head incredulously.

"That was unbelievable. If it's OK with you, I think I'll just go over and knock Alan's teeth down his throat. I'll be back in just a minute."

"That would be fun to watch, but fortunately it will not be necessary. I think Strier is going to have something even better for poor Alan."

"Great. I can't wait to see what he does."

"Look, I have to do some pre-ops. I gotta go. I'll talk to you later."

"Are you sure you're OK?"

"Don't worry. I'm fine. Alan's an asshole. We all knew that."

As I was getting ready to leave, Strier passed by.

"Thanks for coming," he said, putting his hand on my shoulder, "and I really have to apologize. This whole mess here is partly my fault. I had no idea how toxic this place was going to be. I'd do a lot of things differently if I could do it all over again."

"You're about to talk to Alan?"

"I'll talk briefly to him now, but I really don't have much more to say. The next step is to send him over to Roberta. I'm sure he'll enjoy that." This was said ironically. Roberta was very fair, but definitely no-nonsense. Alan was not going to enjoy talking to Roberta at all.

"What will Roberta do?"

Strier shook his head and laughed. "I'm afraid to even think what Roberta might do. I'll tell her what happened here today. I am sure she'll figure out something, and it won't be fun for Alan. He has massively misjudged us. He's about to find that out. I suspect Roberta will want to make an example of him."

"That doesn't sound good at all."

"Not good for Alan, that's for sure. But good for getting everything here moving on an even keel."

I tried to imagine what Roberta might do.

"Alan is in for a shock," Strier said as he moved toward the door where Alan was waiting.

14

The following day I received an email from Strier asking me to stop by. Nothing urgent, but he wanted to keep things moving. I was just starting an eight-hour shift in the ER, so I didn't get to see Strier until the following day.

It was mid-morning when I arrived at his little office in the Laurel Hill anesthesia workroom. As I approached his office door, I suddenly stopped. Right next to Strier's office was another office that was even smaller. The door to the room was closed, but the top half of the door was mostly a large window. Alan Mason was sitting inside reading a book.

The anesthesia workroom had a constant stream of people coming in, staying for a while, and then leaving. Most of them seemed to be glancing in at Alan and sort of smirking as they did so.

Aside from a desk, a chair, and a desktop PC, Alan's little office was empty. The desk was bare. Alan had his legs up and was reading a paperback book. Periodically he glanced out into the anesthesia workroom.

As I stood there, Alan glanced up, saw me, and quickly looked back down at his book.

From his office, Strier saw me standing there and came out to join me. For a moment we both stood about ten feet outside Alan's office door, facing it, watching Alan read.

It was sort of like watching a monkey in a cage at the zoo.

"What the hell is this?" I asked.

"This is Alan's new job," Strier said, watching my reaction

with an amused smile.

"Doing what?"

"Doing nothing."

"What?"

"Alan went over and saw Roberta yesterday," Strier said. "I have no idea what they talked about, but Roberta was seriously displeased. Whatever he said to her was not polite. Not polite at all. So now, like I just said, Alan has a new job."

"Come on, Hank," I said laughing, "you need to tell me more than that. What's going on?"

"Alan's new job is to spend forty hours a week sitting in that office," Strier explained. "Monday through Friday from eight until four thirty, with half an hour for lunch."

"What's he supposed to do?"

"He can bring anything he wants to read. He can surf the internet. He can play video games all day long for all I care."

"And he gets paid?"

"Of course. He has a contract. He gets his full salary. Plus benefits."

"And how long does this last?"

"Until his contract runs out. That happens in three months."

I did some quick mental calculation. "So, basically you're paying Alan one hundred grand to sit in there for three months surfing the internet and reading novels."

"That's it in a nutshell."

"What if he has to go to the bathroom?"

"He gets five minutes for that. Plus lunchtime, of course."

I thought for a minute. "It's sort of like being an animal in a zoo."

"Yeah. Sort of."

"Sort of humiliating."

"He brought this on himself."

"What if he just rebels and refuses to do it?"

"He can certainly quit. We would love that. He can take vacation time. He can take unpaid leave. He might try to call in sick. I'm not sure what we'd do about that."

Strier shrugged.

"But aside from that," he continued, "no, Alan can't just rebel. This is Plan A. If Alan does not conform to Plan A, then we move on to Plan B. I have discussed this with him."

"What's Plan B?"

"I have no idea. That would be up to Roberta. But you can bet that it would be a lot worse than Plan A. Alan understands that he does not want Plan B. Whatever it might be."

"A lot of people would be very happy if you paid them to read novels for three months."

"Exactly."

I did a quick calculation in my head. Alan was earning about two hundred an hour. I watched him for a while. I tried to convince myself that he was earning every penny of it.

We continued to stand there talking, watching Alan read. He clearly knew we were there and was not looking up.

"So, what do you think, Gideon?" Strier asked. "Do you think this will help get this place under control?"

"You really read them the riot act at the M&M conference. That was good. That should help."

"Yes, but that was just words. This is action." Of course, there wasn't much action going on in that little room, but I knew what Strier meant.

"You don't think Roberta will eventually change her mind? Let Alan back into the OR to do cases?"

"Absolutely not. Roberta does not want Alan involved in patient care in any way. She is very concerned after what happened to Arnold last week. That's the main reason she is doing this. Part of it is to discipline Alan. Part of it is to make him an example. But what happened to Arnold is the eight-hundred-pound gorilla in the room. Roberta doesn't want anything even remotely like that happening again."

"Does she think Alan did it? Substituting the syringe?"

"She has no idea. Somebody did. And whoever did it must be pretty familiar with how things work in the OR here. And think about it, Gideon. Even if there was some kind of motive, whoever did that must be at least partially off their rocker."

"Alan seemed a bit off his rocker at the M&M conference."

"That's exactly what Roberta thought when he was over in her office. And she doesn't want anyone who might be off their rocker delivering patient care. Hence no more patient care for Alan."

"Well, she's in charge."

"Yes, and she's ultimately on the line. People will hold her responsible if anything more happens over here."

I could understand that.

But I wanted to switch gears and follow up on something Strier had said earlier.

"The last time we talked," I said, "you said you would do things differently if you had a chance to do it all over again."

"I would. You know, this was my opportunity to run my own show. To take on new challenges. It sounded like fun."

"Not fun, huh?"

"I tried to be low key. I had Dave and Lucy come along because they are both so down-to-earth and friendly. I wanted to put a friendly face on this whole thing."

"I guess it didn't quite work out that way."

"I think it worked for a lot of the people here. But I think people like Alan and Namrata just perceived us as, I don't know, manipulable? Easy to take advantage of? Something like that."

"Or maybe that's just the way they would react to anything. Game the system. Manipulate it, like you just said."

"Maybe. But I clearly have to be much tougher." Strier paused. "Especially after what happened to Arnold."

I thought about it for a moment.

"You know, Dr. Jones laid everything out pretty well in his email. What do you think?"

"You mean the phony email."

"Yes."

"Let's not even talk about that."

"But who did that? I mean, that email was pretty off-the-wall too. Don't we have to think that maybe it was connected? Somehow?"

"Gideon, I just want to run an OR. If I try to think about all that, I'll be the next person around here who goes nuts. Do you think they're connected?"

"I have no idea. But this place just keeps getting weirder and weirder."

I thought for a minute and then I smiled at him.

"I wonder what's next."

15

I guess if you got one phony email, it shouldn't be a big surprise to get two. But the second phony email was a huge surprise to me because it struck much closer to home. In fact, it struck right at home. I was sitting at my home PC at about ten at night when it appeared.

I recognized the sender—Gideon Lowell. *From Me. Great.* This was just what I needed.

Like Jones's phony email, it appeared to be addressed to all the clinical staff at the health system as a whole, plus a bunch of other assorted recipients. The email's subject line said, *The murderer's name is probably on this list.* It had an attachment that I decided I should absolutely not touch. Here's what this little missive had to say:

> *You probably know by now that Dr. James Arnold, the CEO of our health system, died on the operating table and that my wife, Dr. Luciana Rivera, was the anesthesiologist.*
>
> *You may also have heard that we suspect that someone surreptitiously substituted a syringe containing a lethal drug for a syringe containing one of the standard anesthesia drugs that had been prepared for the case. In other words, we strongly suspect that Dr. Arnold was murdered and that my wife was an unknowing participant in this crime.*
>
> *It is almost certain that the murderer is someone*

who works for our health system, and that that person is significantly deranged. To help identify this criminal, I have prepared the attached spreadsheet which contains information produced from our electronic health record.

The spreadsheet lists the names of all health system employees in our electronic medical record system who are currently taking antipsychotic and/or antidepressant medications. These medications and doses are also listed. I have sorted the names so that individuals receiving the highest doses are at the top of the list.

I strongly suspect the murderer's name is on this list and I would not be surprised if it is near the top. Please look at it. Do any of these names bring any issues to mind that you should share with the authorities?

You probably remember the national anthrax scare shortly after 9/11. If someone had prepared a list like this one for Fort Detrick, I suspect that the culprit would have been identified quite rapidly.

I sincerely hope this helps resolve this unfortunate situation.

Gideon Lowell, MD
Department of Emergency Medicine
Boston Central Hospital

Oh great! Terrific!

All I wanted to do was go to bed. How was I ever going to get to sleep after getting this stupid email? Lucy had already gone to bed. The last thing she needed was to have this little pile of shit dumped on her. I was on my own.

I figured the first thing I should do was what Jones had done. So I hit "Reply All" and sent a short message saying that the email had not been sent by me, that it should be deleted, and that the attachment should definitely not be opened.

I absolutely could not look at the attachment. Neither should anybody else. If the email was correct, the attachment contained incredibly sensitive protected health information. Plus, it was potentially libelous. And who knew if it was even accurate? Anyone who opened it could get into a lot of trouble.

I figured the email list I had replied to was probably moderated and that my message probably needed to be electronically approved by somebody before it could be sent out. As a result, I copied individually a whole bunch of people, including my chair, Strier, and everybody else I could think of who knew me reasonably well.

I then went to the health system's IT web page and found a phone number to call in an emergency. I dialed the number and was amazed to find myself talking to an actual human being. I explained what had happened.

She told me that an IT task force would look into it right away. This was the same team that was already working on Jones's phony email. Two members of the task force were still at work despite the fact that it was approaching midnight.

She patched me through, and they understood my problem immediately. They disabled my email account on the spot, and also went to the listserv and approved my message to be sent out. I stupidly tried to see if a copy had come to me, and got a brusque pop-up informing me that my account was no longer active.

This only confirmed that I was basically an idiot. Which I already knew.

I would have to check it on Lucy's email account.

After talking to the task force, I felt a whole lot better. It sounded like people would understand what had happened. I felt I was off the hook—sort of—but it still felt very creepy.

Now what I really needed was sleep. I sat there debating whether I needed to take an Ambien. I finally compromised on half a pill.

Who needs this kind of shit?

16

"Hey, Gideon. You have to come look at this."
It was late in the evening the following day. People had been looking at me strangely all day long, but everybody seemed to understand that I hadn't sent that email.

Lucy and I were at home. We had finally gotten the kids to bed. Maybe they'd stay there and not come wandering back out. Good luck on that. I was relaxing out on our deck, letting the evening fall into twilight around me. Lucy was at the PC in our living room, just a few feet away.

I sort of grunted back at her. I really didn't want to move. "Tell me. What is it?"

"I'm looking at *The Boston World* online. There's an article here by Gwen Swann talking about Arnold's death."

So maybe three seconds later I was right behind my wife, looking at it over her shoulder. The title of the article was "Foul Play Suspected in the Operating Room Death of Dr. James Arnold."

Investigation into the recent death of Dr. James Arnold at Laurel Hill Community Hospital now points to the possibility of foul play. It is suspected that prior to the operation a syringe containing a lethal drug, possibly potassium, may have been substituted for a syringe containing vecuronium, a drug commonly used for anesthesia. The substitute syringe reportedly looked virtually identical to the syringe it replaced and was labeled "Vecuronium."

At the start of the operation, shortly after the drug in that syringe was injected through an intravenous line, Dr. Arnold's heart stopped. Repeated attempts to restart his heartbeat were unsuccessful. Dr. Arnold's death is now being investigated as a suspected criminal act, according to sources with direct knowledge of the investigation.

Dr. Henry Strier, chief of anesthesiology at Laurel Hill Community Hospital, says that potassium is used for open-heart surgery, where the patient's heart is deliberately stopped so that surgery can be performed on the heart itself. When this is done, a very sophisticated pump, called a cardiopulmonary bypass machine, is used to take over the pumping and oxygenation of the patient's blood.

Because of the ongoing criminal investigation, Dr. Strier said that he was unable to comment on the specific circumstances of Dr. Arnold's death. Dr. Strier did say that potassium is never used in normal, non-open-heart procedures, such as the gallbladder operation that was planned for Dr. Arnold. Dr. Strier also said that anesthetic drugs are frequently prepared in advance of a surgical procedure, but that he had never before heard of a syringe being deliberately switched, as is suspected in this case.

The article went on to talk a little about Arnold.

Dr. Arnold was a successful orthopedic surgeon before switching his career focus to health administration. He became CEO of the Boston Central Health System three years ago but continued to perform surgery on a limited basis. He has been an active surgeon at Laurel Hill Community Hospital for over twenty years.

It also talked a bit about the takeover of Laurel Hill Hospital by the health system, for which Arnold was identified as CEO.

Under Dr. Arnold's leadership, Boston Central Health System has been expanding quite rapidly in the past few years, buying up physician practices, clinics, and smaller hospitals in the extended Boston area. Laurel Hill Community Hospital was a recent acquisition.

The most interesting thing to me was what the article didn't say. First of all, it only mentioned Lucy in passing, identifying her as the anesthesiologist who had been involved in the case. It indicated that Lucy really worked at Boston Central Hospital and was working at Laurel Hill Hospital on a temporary basis as part of the takeover. But the article seemed to accept implicitly the theory that a syringe had been deliberately switched, and that Lucy was basically a bystander in a crime.

The article speculated a little about possible motive. It reported that many people at Laurel Hill Hospital had been unhappy with how the takeover was being handled, and that Arnold was perceived as the principal person who had been orchestrating the takeover, describing Arnold as a powerful but "controversial" figure in Boston's medical establishment.

I thought this was great. I gave Lucy a few minutes to read it and digest it. She scrolled up and down a few times, rereading different parts of the article. Finally, I asked, "What do you think?"

"It looks OK. It really doesn't say much."

That sounded like a resounding victory to me.

17

Over the next two days, I talked to a variety of people in the Laurel Hill anesthesia department, and it was not easy. For one thing, it turned out that being deputized didn't mean that people had to talk to me. A real deputy sheriff could throw people in jail. What could I do? Not much. Real deputies had guns and subpoenas. All I had was a stethoscope. Not the same concept.

I tried to talk to four doctors, two nurse anesthetists, and two anesthesia techs. Two of the doctors and one of the nurses basically told me to get lost. They didn't even try to be polite. It was pretty obvious that they were all pissed off about the takeover.

The other two doctors told me they had already spent too much time talking to the police and answering all their interminable questions. But at least they were polite. They answered a few questions. The real problem was they hadn't seen anything, they hadn't heard anything, and they didn't know anything. Sort of like those three monkeys.

The other nurse and the two anesthesia techs actually wanted to help. They answered my questions and they didn't mind sitting there talking for as long as I wanted. But they didn't have much to tell me that related directly to the murder.

I had made up a list of questions that covered the various issues I thought I should ask about. The first thing I wanted to know was whether anyone had seen anything unusual in the operating room area the morning of Arnold's death. No one had. There had been nobody acting suspicious, funny, or strange. Nobody who looked like they didn't belong. Nobody wandering around carrying a syringe.

So much for that.

When I asked about the takeover, none of them were happy with it. But they all knew that takeovers like this were going on all over the country. They agreed that a lot of people at Laurel Hill were angry. I got some names, but they really didn't think any of them were angry enough to start killing people.

When I asked about Arnold's philandering, most of them had heard rumors. But Arnold apparently never philandered with any members of the anesthesia department. Nurses seemed to be his target of opportunity. I got the names of a few nurses who people thought had been involved with Arnold, including two whose husbands were known to have been very upset; one nurse rumored to have had an affair with Arnold committed suicide. Since none of these people were in the anesthesia department, it was unclear how easy it would be for me to find out much more about them.

I did hear some interesting stories. A year or two ago, a surgeon got so angry that he threw a chair out the window of one of the ORs. Nobody knew why. Another surgeon was notorious for angrily insulting everybody in sight when he was doing surgery. But he had done that for years. There were also a lot of stories about confrontations between surgeons and anesthesiologists about particular cases. But I was sure that happened everywhere.

The real question was whether any of this translated into murder. Based on what I heard, I really couldn't imagine anyone in the Laurel Hill anesthesia department being so angry that they concocted and then actually carried out a plan of premeditated murder against Arnold. Unless one of them was seriously off their rocker, which brought up the subject of that spoofed email.

I was, of course, never going to look at the attachment that I supposedly sent out to everybody in the health system—the attachment that ranked everybody in the health system based on the strength of their psychiatric medications. But rumor had it that nobody in the Laurel Hill anesthesia department scored high on that list, which was actually sort of useful to know.

Interestingly, rumor also had it that the surgeon who threw the chair out the OR window scored quite high on the list. I wasn't sure what if anything to make of that.

If there was no hidden anesthesia wacko walking around unknown to everybody, where did that leave me? Well, I had the two emails. Maybe I should focus on them.

18

It was 5:45 in the afternoon and I had just finished wrapping things up after an eight-hour shift in the ER. Wrapping up required that I sit at the computer and type in a whole bunch of detailed information about all the patients I had seen, an excruciating process. Life was much simpler when we just used paper.

Fortunately, the patients had not been too complicated. But it was late summer, and that meant I was supervising residents who were just out of medical school, so I had to be careful. It would be easy for them to miss things. But they were smart, and it was fun to teach them.

I was now in the Washington Room of the Boston Public Library, at one of their free internet stations. A large painting of George Washington aiming a cannon in my general direction was on the back wall. The room had clearly been designed for something other than computers. The ceiling was about three times higher than it needed to be. The computer setup was pretty odd too. They emerged out of large, dark rectangular tables like mushrooms sprouting from fallen tree trunks deep in the forest. It must have been somebody's idea of an ergonomic design. I'd never seen anything like it.

I had decided the internet might be a good place to look for clues. I was doing it in the main city library so I wouldn't leave digital footprints that linked to my home PC or to any PC at the hospital. My goal was to stay in the shadows as much as possible—*sub rosa*.

My main question was who sent those emails. Whoever it was had to have quite intimate knowledge of what was going on at Laurel Hill Hospital. He (or she) had to have access to the anesthesiology M&M handouts, which were supposed to be confidential. He or she also had to be very sophisticated about computer technology and have access to Laurel Hill Hospital and to the health system's electronic patient records. Maybe Google could help. It contained a mammoth amount of information.

I had made a list of search terms. These included the obvious—*Laurel Hill Community Hospital, anesthesiology, morbidity and mortality, computer spoofing, information technology,* and so on. I also included a bunch of names, for example Alan Mason and Namrata. I had tried to cast the net widely in making up the list.

I entered the various search terms, pairing them up systematically to see what I could find. After about a half an hour I was nowhere and getting bored. I looked at pages and pages of uninteresting stuff, like hospitals that had technology and numbers to contact for further information (when I entered Laurel Hill Community Hospital and information technology). Or I got caller ID spoofing at a Laurel Hill School Association located somewhere in the Midwest (when I entered Laurel Hill Community Hospital and email spoofing). Clearly no help.

I next tried people's names, starting with Namrata. Right off the bat, I found a long list of women named Namrata, including some who were famous Indian actresses. Two of them had been in movies I had seen, although I had absolutely no recollection that they had been named Namrata. I spent a few minutes looking at pictures of gorgeous Indian women all named Namrata. All that long, flowing dark hair and those beautiful eyes. I suddenly thought, *Wow. Namrata must be a glamorous name in India.*

Who knew?

Then I started pairing Namrata's full name, Namrata Sharma, with other terms from my list. Pairing Namrata Sharma with mortality and morbidity brought up a whole bunch of Doctor Namratas, but nothing useful.

When I tried Namrata Sharma and computer science,

however, I finally hit pay dirt. It was an engagement announcement posted on what looked like an alumni website for some kind of technical high school in Bangalore, India. It was written in English. The whole website was in English. It announced that Vikram Sastri (the alumnus) was engaged to be married to Dr. Namrata Sharma. It then described the happy couple. There was no photo, but it was clear that this was the correct Namrata. She had an MBBS from a medical school in New Delhi (the Indian equivalent of an MD), had training in anesthesiology in India and in the US, and was currently working in Boston.

Bingo.

But Vikram was the really interesting one. He had an undergraduate degree and a PhD, both in computer science and both from the Indian Institute of Technology in Bangalore (the Indian equivalent of MIT). He was currently working as a computer consultant in the US.

And there was more. The announcement must have been placed by Vikram's proud parents. Reading somewhat between the lines, it described how his parents had seen a description of Namrata that her parents posted on an Indian matrimonial website. Vikram's parents immediately became very excited because Namrata was working in the same US hospital as their son. It didn't say which one, but it clearly had to be Laurel Hill Hospital.

They had contacted Namrata's parents, who lived in New Delhi, in northern India. (Vikram's family lived in Bangalore in southern India.) The two sets of parents must then have checked each other out in some detail. The announcement did not say how they did it.

I was really impressed. It sounded like a great way to meet a potential spouse. This was definitely not about arranged marriages. It was about arranged introductions to appropriate people whom you probably had a lot in common with. It sounded light-years better than Match.com.

In any case, mutual approval had clearly ensued, and both offspring were contacted. The offspring in turn contacted each other and the rest was history.

Needless to say, this was a spectacular find. I printed out the engagement announcement as well as the Google search page that found it. Now I had to find out more about Vikram.

But first I had to go home, have dinner, and help put the kids to bed.

19

Rachael Ward was a nurse who worked on quality of care for Laurel Hill Hospital and in the process worked a lot with computers. She seemed like a good person to start asking questions about IT without being too obvious. A clinical person who worked with computers. I didn't want to go directly to someone in IT. I wanted to stay under the radar.

The next morning, I arrived at Rachael's office at the appointed hour of ten, which we had agreed to by email. My email was still shut down, so I used my wife's. I brought along a list of five people who worked for IT at Laurel Hill Hospital according to the hospital directory. I had also put Vikram's name on the list. He had not been in the directory. My goal was to learn more about Vikram, but I wanted to disguise this by asking about several other people at the same time. I wanted to know if Vikram was sophisticated enough to have sent those emails.

I introduced myself, which drew a big smile and a friendly laugh.

"Hello, Gideon. It is a pleasure to meet you." I knew that smile. It was my name. I think my name helped break the ice with a lot people. I had yet to meet another person named Gideon. If I ever did, it would be a singular event.

"Rachael," I said.

Her office was a little museum of memorabilia, with about fifteen pictures on one wall and a bunch of athletic trophies on the shelves of her bookcases. There was also a gold-plated softball mounted on a plaque sitting prominently on the left front corner of her desk. Presumably some kind of championship trophy. I gestured to it.

"What position did you play?"

"Pitcher," she replied. She said it proudly. "I always played pitcher."

I believed her. She had the build for it, about five-eleven, long, limber, and athletic. I noticed that her right arm was significantly more muscular than her left.

Her straight brown hair was in a ponytail. I looked at one of the pictures on the wall and saw a tall, thin young girl in her teens with the same ponytail standing in the center of a team of smiling young women. Presumably a softball team. She was now about fifteen years older but didn't look that much different.

"Thank you for agreeing to talk to me," I said.

"No problem."

"As I indicated in my email, the Department of Anesthesiology has asked me to help them sort out what is going on. Right now, I am focusing on the two emails. I obviously have a personal interest in trying to figure out who might possibly have sent them."

"I don't know if I can help, but I'm happy to do what I can."

I started with a random name at the top of my list. Someone I was not interested in. The only person I cared about was Vikram. But if nothing else, I figured I'd learn more about Laurel Hill Hospital by asking about a bunch of other people.

"Bradley Stratton," I said.

"I know Brad."

"What's he like?"

"Around forty. Married. Three kids. He has a master's in health science. He manages the Laurel Hill Hospital clinical information systems. He's a nice guy. And even more important, he has excellent taste in women."

She waited for me to react to that one.

"Oh?"

"He's married to a nurse."

I laughed. "Ah hah. Good for him. I bet that actually helps him a lot in his work."

"I think so," she agreed. "So, what do you want to know about Brad?"

"How technical is he? I mean, does he just manage IT? Does he write code?"

"I don't think Brad does any programming. He just coordinates everything and makes sure the systems run. He also spends a lot of time analyzing software. Deciding what to buy."

"He doesn't sound like someone who could have sent those emails, even if he wanted to," I said.

"I agree. And he would have absolutely no reason to do it."

I suspected motive was going to be a big issue for all of the IT people on my list. The lack of any apparent motive, that is.

"What about you, Rachael? Do you program the computer?" It hadn't occurred to me to put her on the list, but she had two large computer screens on her desk, which sort of indicated that she was more than just a casual user.

"Oh yes indeed, I absolutely program the computer. It's mostly what I do. Getting data out of the patient record system, organizing it, analyzing it. That's my job. I program all the time."

"Oh really."

"Yes. For example, I could easily have compiled that list of all those people and their psych meds. That list that you, Gideon, sent around to everybody in sight."

"Of course, that wasn't me. You must know that."

"You know, if it had just been that single email, I think people would not have known what to think. But it came right after that first email, supposedly from Dr. Jones, that was so clearly over the top. It's pretty obvious that someone is playing games with us. So no, I don't believe anybody thinks you sent it. Why in the world would you? It would make no sense."

I hoped she was right—that everyone did indeed assume I hadn't done it. It seemed to be the case.

"So, how did you get into computers, Rachael?"

"Years ago, I dated a computer programmer. He got me started. Nursing is fine, but I needed something more. I wound up getting a master's degree in informatics from Oregon. Online."

"So you enjoy it."

"It fits perfectly with all the nursing I used to do."

I thought about this for a moment and then decided to have some fun.

"OK, Rachael, so tell me, how would you go about spoofing email? Assuming that you wanted to."

She clearly thought this was an amusing question.

"Let's see. Hmmm." She was laughing. "Say I wanted to send out an email from Dr. Jones, for example. Is that the type of thing you mean?"

"Yeah. Just as a completely hypothetical example."

"Well, I think all the passwords are encrypted, so I couldn't just look them up in a database somewhere. I guess someone could put a keystroke recorder on Jones's computer, but I have no idea how to do that."

"Anything else?"

"Yes. Doctors are terrible at remembering passwords. So they write them down. Sometimes right on the desk next to their computers. Can you believe that? What a bunch of dummies. Or else on a piece of paper in a drawer of their desk. I would sneak into Jones's office and try to find his password."

"OK, so that's how you got Jones's password. How did you get mine?"

"Oh, yours was a bit more difficult." She smiled.

"But not impossible?"

"No, actually, I would have no idea how to get yours. You have a computer background, don't you, Gideon? You probably use a strong password and never write it down."

She was pretty close. If I didn't write something down, I would for sure eventually forget it. But she would have to pick my pocket, not just look in my desk. And I didn't write down the whole password, just the part I changed periodically.

"How did you know about my computer background?"

"Someone said you *could* have sent that email if you wanted to."

"I don't know about that," I said. "But I did do computer programming for industry for several years. My specialty was real-time multi-threaded process control. It paid well, but I wound up sitting in front of a computer at least eight hours a day. Usually a lot more."

"You did the opposite of me. You went from computers into medicine."

"I sure did."

"Why medicine?"

"You really want to know?"

"Sure. Please."

"It's sort of a funny story."

"Then I definitely want to hear it."

"Well, I had a dream. Literally. I was working out off Route 128 in aerospace. One night I dreamed that I was in some funny area in downtown Boston. It was evening. Everything was gray. There were big concrete buildings all around. Parking garages. Office buildings that had closed for the night. But I was very happy. And guess why?"

"I have absolutely no idea."

"Because I was in medical school. I have no idea what it all meant. But I woke up in the middle of the night. And lying there in bed I was incredibly depressed and disappointed because I realized I was actually not in medical school. I was still just programming stupid computers out on Route 128."

"Based on that, you decided to go to medical school?"

"I started applying the next morning. I had already taken all the required courses."

"And the rest is history?"

"And the rest *is* history."

She laughed. "Well, welcome to medicine at Laurel Hill Hospital."

"Thanks. And I do have a bunch of further questions."

I started in on some of the other names on my list.

Who they were? What were they like? What were their skills? Did she think they could conceivably have sent the emails? And if not, why not? Her answer was always no, she didn't think any of them did it, for multiple reasons. No knowledge of anesthesiology. No apparent motive. Insufficient technical skills to spoof email.

What really struck me was how quickly she seemed to pick up on the nuances of all the questions I was asking.

Then I got to Vikram. His name seemed to take her a bit by surprise.

"I do know Vikram, but not well. He doesn't work for Laurel Hill Hospital. He's a consultant."

"What does he do?"

"They brought him in to help with the billing fiasco. He's been here for almost a year."

"The billing fiasco?"

"You haven't heard about our billing fiasco? Where have you been?" She said that laughing, but with pretend shock as if I was a total idiot. "A year and a half ago they put in a new billing system for all clinical care at Laurel Hill Hospital. It immediately messed everything up and we lost millions of dollars."

Actually, I had heard something about this from Lucy, but it hadn't really registered. It happened well before the takeover. "What was the problem?"

"Well, I just know what I hear. I'm not an expert in accounting, but apparently the system they put in was a so-called balance forward system. For each patient, it records every bill you send out and every payment that comes in. But that's basically all."

"And that's a problem?"

"Well, a typical bill gets paid partly by Medicare, for example, partly by an insurance company, partly by the patient, and partly not paid at all. A balance forward system doesn't keep track of any of that. It just keeps track of the bottom line. It doesn't link each bill to the payments. And a sick patient can have hundreds of separate bills."

"So, there was no way of knowing what was going on."

"Nobody could figure out what had been paid and what hadn't been paid."

"How can people be so stupid? To put in a system like that, I mean."

"We're a hospital. We're good at patient care. We're not good at everything. I think that was partly why we got taken over." She shrugged.

"And Vikram was supposed to fix this?"

"Vikram did fix it. Vikram is amazing. He created a parallel system that keeps track of everything. He wrote it all in three months. All by himself. It now requires twice as much work to enter everything into both computer systems, but now at least they can usually figure out what is going on."

"So, Vikram is very skilled."

"Yes, Vikram is in a completely different league than any of the other computer people here at Laurel Hill Hospital, several levels more sophisticated." She paused. "And he definitely knows it. He is very smart and he's not afraid to let you know he's a lot smarter than you are."

"You think he could have written those emails and sent them out like that?"

"You got me. If anyone around here could, I bet he could. But I really don't know what's involved." She paused again. "You think he might have done it?"

"Somebody did it."

"But does it make any sense? I mean, why would he do it? What's the incentive? He doesn't even work at the hospital. He's here temporarily. And he's got to be really well paid. It would make no sense at all for him to do something like that."

"You are probably right. I guess it really has to be someone much more closely connected to the hospital." I was backpedaling; no point in tipping my hand any more than I had to.

Well, I had what I came for. This was clearly enough about Vikram. So, I asked her about a couple more IT people on my list and then started wrapping things up.

It was pretty clear to me that Vikram must have sent those emails. Something Namrata told him must have sent him off the deep end. Computer people did weird things. And they did those weird things for weird reasons. After four years at MIT and three years doing system programming for the aerospace industry, I knew that firsthand.

Now I had to figure out what to do about Vikram.

As I was getting ready to leave, Rachael seemed pensive, as if she was holding something back. I leaned back in my chair and tried to project the image of a friendly big brother.

"What's up, Rachael? Is there something more?"

She finally spoke, looking as if it was perhaps against her better judgment. "Just before he was killed, I was doing a project for Dr. Arnold on cardiac surgery outcomes at Laurel Hill Hospital."

"They're good, right? Laurel Hill Hospital has a top program in cardiac surgery."

"Laurel Hill Hospital has a very good reputation for doing bread and butter cardiac procedures. Like cardiac bypass surgery. Dr. Arnold was thinking maybe he should build it up. Make Laurel Hill Hospital a center of excellence for cardiac surgery within the health system as a whole."

"In fact, he had his own bypass surgery here. Is that right?"

"He did." She said, looking at me uncertainly.

"Yes?" I ventured.

"Can I show you something strange?"

"Please do."

She sat at her desk in front of the two large monitors. She gestured for me to bring my chair up beside her.

She opened up what looked like an electronic patient record and paged around in it from one screen to another, eventually winding up with two black-and-white images showing ribs, lungs, and a heart, one image on each screen.

"Look at these closely and tell me if you see anything unusual." She moved her chair off to the side so I could get a better look. "The image on the left is Dr. Arnold's chest X-ray from earlier this year. Do you see anything unusual?"

I looked it over, starting with the bones and the peripheral aspects, and then the heart and lungs. You need to make sure you don't just focus on the lungs, for example, and miss an incidental metastatic cancer in the humerus. "It looks pretty normal to me." I said. "Obviously he had heart surgery." There were wire loops that had been put in to hold the sternum together after his bypass operation. This X-ray was probably a routine follow-up film.

"Of course, I am not an expert in all the subtleties of reading chest X-rays," I said.

"Now look at this. This is Dr. Arnold's cath film. An angiogram." She reached over and clicked on the image of a heart, which started to beat as soon as she clicked, contracting and expanding rhythmically like a heart is supposed to do. The film showed contrast dye being squirted into the coronary arteries that provided blood to the heart muscle itself. Here I was totally out of my depth. It presumably showed blockages that needed to be fixed.

"I am not an expert in this at all," I said. "Maybe these two arteries are occluded?" I pointed to two places where maybe the arteries appeared to be narrowed.

"Forget about the arteries," Rachael said. "Look at the rest of the image. And compare it with this one." She gestured at the chest X-ray.

I looked at them, going back and forth. "Well, the angiogram image obviously doesn't have the wires in." I glanced at her. "But that's no big surprise. The angiogram was done before the operation."

"Right," she said. "Keep looking."

I looked back and forth and finally pointed to a small grayish area in one of the ribs in the chest X-ray. "I don't see this little blemish on the cath film. But maybe it just didn't show up."

"Dr. Arnold said it should have shown up. He got speared in the chest falling onto a lacrosse stick in high school. It cracked his rib. No big deal. It probably hurt like hell for a month or two and then healed by itself. But you can still just barely see where it happened."

"So, why doesn't it show on the angiogram?"

"You tell me. What do you think?"

"Like I said, it's a different imaging technique. Maybe the angiogram image is just not as sensitive. It's not designed for bones."

"That's a reasonable thought, but it's apparently not the case. It should show up. Why else?"

I thought for a minute. There was only one thing I could think of. I glanced at Rachael. She was smiling, and I guess that she could tell what I was thinking.

"It's not his film."

"Exactly. It's someone else's angiogram."

"Do you know whose?"

"I have no idea. But the funny thing is Dr. Arnold had a cardiac surgeon look at it and the pathology is very similar to Arnold's. It pretty much matches the written report. Dr. Arnold had some imaging experts start investigating this in detail. A group of outside consultants. He got them started doing this a few days before he died. I think they are looking at all Laurel Hill Hospital's recent angiogram images. We are waiting for their report."

"Do you have any idea what they might find?"

"I called them up this morning. They apparently have a big cluster in the cloud, whatever that means, comparing each angiogram image that we have with every other image that we have. And they are finding multiple duplicates based on the images."

"So, the database is all messed up?"

"It's worse than that. They told me that apparently the metadata has been altered so that the images appear to match up with the patient whose chart it is linked to. By metadata they mean the patient ID, the date, and stuff like that."

"That sounds deliberate."

"It sounds deliberate."

"Uh-oh," I said with a smile.

She looked at me. "Gideon, you have summed it up very concisely. Uh-oh, indeed."

"So when will you know for sure what they find?"

"Maybe next week. That's what they told me. Once I get the report, I need to figure out who to give it to. Arnold ordered it, but now he's dead."

"Can I come back and talk to you about it next week?"

"That would be fine. I'll let you know by email when I hear anything."

"Assuming they restore my email account."

"If they don't, give me a call."

As I headed out the door, I said it again with a laugh. "Uh-oh." I liked the sound of it.

"Uh-oh, for sure," she said. "See you next week."

20

The next afternoon, I sat in the waiting room of the Laurel Hill Hospital Office of Risk Management. I had never been to an office of risk management before. This was apparently where the Laurel Hill Hospital lawyers hung out. I was not sure how many of them there were. Maybe just one. Maybe two or three. Who knew?

I really didn't know what they did, either. Their main job must be to ride herd on all the lawsuits that patients brought against the hospital. If we were automobiles, we'd just get tossed in the junkyard once we started to get old and decrepit. Since we were people, modern medicine tried to keep us going as long as it could. But that often didn't work out as planned. Plus, of course, doctors did make mistakes. Hence the need for risk management.

Cold-blooded murder in the operating room was probably not something they had to deal with very frequently.

Strier sent me an email the day before, telling me that we had been "summoned." That's how he phrased it. They gave us a time to appear, which happened to be convenient for both of us, so here we were. Neither of us had any idea what this was all about.

We had an appointment to talk to Ebenezer Clarke, JD, who turned out to be a kid in his late twenties who called himself Ben. How the heck did anybody get named Ebenezer these days anyway? But then, who was a guy named Gideon to talk?

Ben led us into his office and seated us around a small table. One of the seats was already occupied. Ben introduced us.

"This is Detective Glenn Santoro from the Boston Police Department. He is working on the Arnold case."

Detective Santoro smiled in an easy, relaxed manner, almost as if the world amused him, and since we were part of the world, we amused him too. Looking at him, it occurred to me that he had probably seen people do a lot of crazy things, and this must be his way of taking it all in stride.

Santoro looked to be in his late thirties, about my age. He looked fit without being overly muscular and about six feet tall. He had a round, totally bald head and a light-brown mustache. Whereas Ben was wearing a suit and tie, Santoro was wearing khaki slacks and a light-tan pull-over jersey. He looked very comfortable.

As soon as he opened his mouth, I realized that my hopes of flying under the radar with my investigation had been a fantasy.

"Ah, Sherlock Holmes and Dr. Watson, I presume. It's a real pleasure to meet you." He continued to smile, and I think there was an actual twinkle in his eye.

How was I supposed to respond to this? I couldn't think of a thing to say. Fortunately, Strier was up to the challenge.

"It's a pleasure to meet you. I assume we are here to talk about Dr. Arnold. We are happy to do anything we can to help."

Santoro leaned back and smiled indulgently. Like a favorite uncle talking to two nephews in need of a little friendly advice.

"Actually, your help is exactly what we are here to talk about. I am not sure how much help we really need." Santoro continued to smile as if he was thinking, *OK, so what are these two clowns going to try to pull next?*

As Detective Santoro said this, a whole lot of thoughts started swirling around in my head. For one thing, I thought maybe I could find out how the investigation was going, at least as far as Lucy was concerned. But much more significantly, it sounded like the hospital and the police were about to do their best to quash any questioning by Strier and myself.

"I guess I'm not exactly sure what you're saying," I said. "Maybe we could step back a little and you could give us a little context, a little bit of overview, as to why we are here. I know you have already talked extensively to Hank here about what happened. About the event."

"I'd be happy to." Santoro grinned. "We are here because the Boston Police Department is conducting a murder investigation. In the course of our investigation, we will be asking people lots of questions. We are meeting today to make sure you understand that the two of you can't be running around doing your own investigation at the same time."

He stopped and looked at both of us in turn, presumably giving us each a chance to ask questions. Then he continued.

"That's not the way it works. In the first place, if you do your own investigation, it will confuse people. It could also be perceived as trying to influence people's stories. Or even to intimidate them."

"So, if we talk to people, it interferes with your investigation." I was perhaps stating the obvious, but "talking to people" is pretty broad. Where does "talking to people" end and "investigating" start? That was my real question, but I really didn't want to push him too hard about it. What was the point? He'd just repeat what he just said.

"Yes," he said. "In fact, there are laws about that. There are legal penalties. I am assuming that it won't come to this, but if necessary, we can arrest people who interfere with our investigation and bring charges against them."

There it was, spelled out, face up on the table. But I had a lot of trouble imagining that would ever actually happen.

"And what about Ben here? What about the hospital lawyers?" I asked. I looked at Ben. "What's your role in all this?"

"It's very simple," he said. "Our mission is to protect the hospital and to protect its employees. We do that all the time. When an adverse event occurs, we talk to the people involved. We gather information so that we understand what happened. Then we decide what to do. But of course, this case is not typical. Since this is a criminal investigation, we have to step back. The police investigate and we cooperate with them in any way they ask us to."

Strier sat arms folded across his chest, seeming like he was ready to burst. He cleared his throat.

"I do understand the basic point, but look at it from my perspective for a minute. A murder has occurred in the workplace that I am responsible for. For me, that is very scary because I have no idea why it occurred. If I knew for sure that this was a one-time event, that someone wanted Dr. Arnold dead, and that's it, then what you say makes perfect sense. But how do we know that? What if there is a nut loose in the Laurel Hill Hospital operating rooms and another patient gets killed? I really have to do my best to make sure that doesn't happen."

"Yes, and my understanding is that you have taken a lot of steps to try to make sure it doesn't happen again," Ben said, glancing at Santoro. "Also, as you know, we have put up quite a few new video monitors in all the OR areas. Some you can see. Some are hidden. You won't see those even if you look for them. If we see anything, we will let you know right away."

"OK," Strier relented, "but think about it for a minute. Everybody's talking about this. I have to continue to interact with my staff. Are you saying I can't talk to them about any of this?"

"Conversation is fine," Santoro said, "but don't investigate. I think you know what I mean. And if you do hear anything that might be helpful, please let us know."

Ben chimed in. "If you have any questions, just call me. Here's my cell phone." He handed us each his business card with his cell number hand-written on the back.

I decided there was nothing to be gained by trying to push this, so I changed the subject, speaking now to Santoro.

"Yesterday, Dr. Namrata Sharma came barging into Strier's office over in the OR area when Lucy and I were there talking to him and started screaming at Lucy. Saying Lucy had told the police that she, Namrata, had switched the syringe. Namrata was screaming at Lucy and calling her very nasty names."

"I heard about that," Santoro said. "I really can't discuss anything your wife told me, but you can certainly ask her. I can assure you, though, that that is not what your wife told us."

I nodded. "Since you were here, I thought I might mention that."

At this point Santoro shifted so that he was facing me, and then smiled.

"So, tell me about your name."

"My name? OK, my name. Well, my father decided to name me after one of my ancestors. Captain Gideon Lowell. He was sort of a pirate back in the early 1700s. My father was a bit eccentric."

"I mean your last name. Lowell is a well-known Boston name."

"You mean as in 'Lowells speak only to Cabots and Cabots speak only to God'?"

"Yes. That. Exactly."

"That's a completely different branch of the family."

I could see where he was going now.

"I'm descended from a bunch of farmers, merchants, and sailors who lived in southern Maine. I have a whole lot of second and third cousins up in the Portland area."

"I see. So, I don't have to worry that you are somehow heavily politically connected."

That was what this was about.

"No. I am not politically connected at all. Not to worry."

We all talked a bit longer, but the basic message had been communicated. We were not to interfere with the police investigation by trying to investigate on our own. But as I thought that through, it seemed to me that it still left us with a considerable amount of wiggle room.

I'd still try to do everything I could completely *sub rosa*. The rest of the time I would apparently have to wiggle.

I thought about it for a minute.

Wiggling sounded fun.

What could he do to me? I mean, come on. Really.

21

My subconscious mind must have been ruminating about Lucy's sock on that Laurel Hill Hospital bulletin board. It jolted me awake at around three in the morning. I grabbed my bedside notepad and jotted down, *Maybe the sock had not been stolen!*

The following day I decided to explore this further.

I tried to remember where on the web I had purchased all those silly socks for my wife. I had placed several orders over the past few years—for Christmas, for Valentine's Day, for her birthday. For fun, basically. They had a wide variety of styles. It was a lot of fun to go to their website and order a few pairs.

I couldn't remember the exact name, but I usually keep receipts. After about five minutes of shuffling through piles of receipts and printouts, I couldn't find anything.

So, I turned to the internet searching for things like *silly women's socks, funny women's socks, and peculiar women's socks.* Finally, I found a website called Exotic Socks with pictures of several pairs that I had given to Lucy over the years. One of them matched the one that had been pinned up on the Laurel Hill bulletin board.

The website gave an address in London and a phone number. It was nine thirty in the morning in Boston, which made it roughly mid-afternoon there. I dialed the number and got a young woman with a charming British accent.

"Exotic Socks. May I be of help?"

"Hi," I said, "I'm calling from the United States. I've purchased your socks for my girlfriend several times. I am trying to remember exactly what I ordered. Can you help me?"

"Certainly, sir. Could you give me your email address?"

I gave it to her and within a moment or two she had pulled up a record of my purchases.

"Yes, Gideon, you have been a steady customer. During the past three years, you have purchased our socks on five separate occasions."

"*Jolly good!*" I said, waiting for a friendly reaction. Nothing. "Could you email me a copy of those receipts?"

"Certainly. Let me put you on hold for just a bit."

A moment later she returned.

"All complete."

I opened up my email—no longer blocked—and watched her five messages materialize. This was great, but this was not why I had called. I was just softening her up, making her feel comfortable with me, Gideon Lowell, the steady customer—a thoroughly trustworthy individual. Now came the punch line.

"That's terrific," I said. "Thanks a lot. I have one more request."

"Please."

"I am planning to buy some more socks. I always do it from your web page. But I think my girlfriend recently ordered some herself. I want to make sure I don't order the same thing. Could you check for me?"

"No problem at all. What is her email address?"

So I gave her Namrata's email address. This was what I had called for. I was fishing, but this was my hunch. It didn't take long.

"Yes, I have her order right here. It was just last month. She only ordered one pair."

Jackpot.

"Can you tell me which style?" I asked. "Or maybe the catalog number?"

She gave me the number. It matched.

"And could you email me the receipt? That way I can keep everything all together."

"No problem."

Within seconds, Namrata's order appeared in my inbox. I said, "Thanks a lot" and got a peppy "Cheerio" in reply.

This was great. I now had Namrata nailed to the wall.

Namrata's order was in an attachment. It listed her name and email address. It had the date of purchase. It had the item number from the catalog.

I was now loaded for bear. I had everything I needed to blast Namrata right out into the open where everyone could see what she had done. The only question now was how to do it. I thought about giving the printouts to Strier and letting him decide what to do.

But I finally decided I should let the punishment fit the crime. I waited until evening. I had to help Lucy put the kids to bed, so I didn't get to it until ten, but that was fine. The Laurel Hill OR suite would be largely deserted.

I printed off a copy of Namrata's order. I then went to the Exotic Socks website and brought up a picture of that exact pair of socks, including the item number. I printed a copy of that too. The only gloves I had at home were winter gloves. I put on a pair and collected the printouts from the printer. No point in leaving fingerprints. I put on a white medical jacket and drove over to Laurel Hill.

Ten minutes after I arrived, the two printouts were tacked up on the bulletin board in the exact same location where, according to Freeman, the offending sock had been found.

I didn't see anyone in the OR area at all. The day shift had long since gone home. The evening call team was either elsewhere in the hospital or inside one or more ORs doing emergency cases. There were assorted people wandering the halls outside the OR, but I doubted that anyone noticed me. If you wore a white coat and looked like you knew what you were doing, you could go almost anywhere in a hospital, and nobody paid attention as long as you stayed out of highly specialized areas.

I had posted the two printouts on the bulletin board without any kind of note saying what they were. They were self-explanatory: a picture of the socks, and the invoice showing that Namrata had purchased them a few weeks ago. I figured that would be enough.

Now I just had to wait.

22

The next day I went over to talk to Strier. I had a few more questions I could ask him, but mainly I wanted to see if my nighttime visit had stirred up anything interesting. Apparently it had.

"Hi, Gideon," Strier greeted me as I walked into his little office. "Did you hear that the tooth fairy left something on our bulletin board last night?"

"The tooth fairy?" I asked.

"Yes, the tooth fairy. You wouldn't know anything about that, would you?" He was smiling.

"Me?" I said. I had trouble keeping a straight face.

"I believe the tooth fairy was a bit over six feet tall. Thin. Dark hair. Glasses. . . . Ring a bell?"

"Oh, did someone see this tooth fairy?" I asked in feigned innocence.

Strier said nothing. He just sat there looking at me with a somewhat amused but otherwise unreadable expression. I suddenly remembered that he played in a regular poker game. It was like he had just raised the bet and was being careful not to let anyone know if he really had the cards or not.

Well, OK. I had read Mike Caro's book on poker tells. I could play this game. I smiled back at him in a friendly, noncommittal fashion and didn't say anything either. It was clear that he was pretty sure I had done it, but without evidence it was just his gut feeling.

I wondered if Laurel Hill Hospital had security video of people going in and out through the main lobby. I made a mental note to look, but I knew I'd forget.

Finally, Strier spoke. "Do you know what was posted?"

"Lucy called me this morning," I said. "Apparently Namrata ordered the sock that got pinned to the bulletin board."

"Yes. That was very helpful, Gideon. That the tooth fairy posted all that information on the bulletin board for us, I mean."

I still wasn't going to acknowledge anything. Mind games.

"What happens now?" I asked.

"Namrata is going over to talk to Roberta later this afternoon. I set it all up. Roberta knows what happened."

"What do you think she'll do?" I asked.

"Well, Alan only insulted Lucy verbally and just in front of our department. What Namrata did by posting that sock and that note was much more pernicious. I can't imagine she will be doing any more patient care. I suspect that Roberta will request Namrata's resignation and threaten some kind of disciplinary action if Namrata refuses. Actually, *threaten* is not the correct word. *Promise*. Roberta will promise disciplinary action."

"So, one way or another Namrata is history?"

"No more patient care," Strier said. "I guarantee that. We can't have wacko people delivering patient care in our ORs. Not after what happened with Arnold."

"But Namrata won't have to sit in a little office like Alan?"

"One person doing that is enough. It makes the point. We don't need Namrata around at all, and this business with the sock completely seals the deal as far as I'm concerned. If she doesn't resign, it will not be pleasant for her at all. And she's not stupid. I'll bet she resigns. But one way or another, she's gone."

"That will make Lucy very happy. This removes the whole issue of that stupid sock and it removes Namrata at the same time."

"Two birds with one stone, huh?" Strier smiled.

I laughed. "Hank. I am shocked. Birds are proud animals. Calling Namrata a bird is an insult to an entire species. To an entire family of species."

"I'll apologize to the next bird I see," Strier promised. "Anyway, I think this moves this place one big step closer to sanity."

"So, what now?"

"Well, like I said yesterday, our number one priority is that there be no more murders in any of our ORs."

"And number two?" I asked.

Strier shrugged.

"Number two is to figure out who killed Arnold," he continued, "if at all possible. And hopefully it turns out to be someone who has no connection at all with this anesthesia department."

"Actually, I am working on that," I said. "There were some other things going on just before Arnold was killed. I should know a lot more next week."

"I guess I can wait," Strier said, "and incidentally, I should tell you that virtually everybody here assumes you posted those printouts on the bulletin board. If you didn't, I'd really like to know who did."

I thought about this and decided I might as well officially confess.

"Well," I said, "let's just say that your description of the tooth fairy was remarkably accurate."

"I figured. Thanks."

"But please don't share that with anybody else."

"Even Lucy?" he asked.

"I'll tell Lucy. She was asleep last night when I did it. When the tooth fairy did it, that is."

Then a thought occurred to me.

"But how do you know it was really the tooth fairy? We can't just go jumping to conclusions and pointing fingers. We need to cover all the angles. Maybe it was the Easter Bunny. What do you think?"

"It's late summer, Gideon. It wasn't the Easter Bunny."

"OK. Tooth fairy. Fine."

Maybe the Easter Bunny could help us with something else.

23

was walking along the banks of the Charles River near the Hatch Shell with Yuri Marin, one of my classmates from MIT.

Yuri had always been a happy little nerd with an infectious smile, a gleam in his eye, and, even after all these years, a bounce in his step when he got excited.

Back in college, Yuri was rail thin, but now he was rotund and balding, with close-cut dark hair that already showed a sprinkling of early gray. He had grown a bit in height in his late teens and was now about five foot seven. To Yuri, technology was a big sandbox, and he was always finding new toys to play with. He worked for a large, mysterious computer consulting company named IntelliSciTech Systems, which had a major presence just north of Boston. I knew that IntelliSciTech did some consulting for Boston Central Health System on cybersecurity and thought he might be able to help.

"You must know why I wanted to talk to you," I said to my old friend.

"It's those world-famous emails, right?"

"Exactly. What do you know about them?"

"Not a whole lot, but I did ask around at work. I know there are two of them. And one of them claims you as its author. That's the one with the attachment that is totally freaking everybody out. I'm not surprised it's freaking people out."

"I never opened it," I said. "If it really does have a list of people sorted based on the strength of their psychiatric medications, that's obviously incredibly private information."

"But pretty much anyone could have done it, right? Technically, I mean. They would just need to have access."

"I would think you'd need to have some basic understanding of medicine," I said. "Technically, I agree. It's pretty simple if you have access to the patient record. But you need to have some kind of table comparing the strength of all the different psychiatric medications. You'd probably need to make up that table yourself."

"People are definitely very upset." He paused. "Oh, I forgot. Did you hear about the senator?"

"The senator?"

"One of the people on that list is the daughter of a US senator."

"Oh no. I hadn't heard anything about that."

"She's a clinical psychologist, and she's bipolar. Apparently, you can tell that from her meds."

"That's not good at all."

"Yup. And when a senator calls up the CEO of a big health system that has released personal psychiatric information about his daughter, things have a way of transitioning into a totally different dimension."

"Of course, he can't call up a dead CEO," I quipped.

"Come on, Gideon, you know what I mean. So now, everybody's going crazy. Covering their asses. Pointing fingers at everybody else. Of course, they don't do all that right out in plain sight. But they're doing it all the same. It's a big mess."

"All because of the senator?"

"Yes. Absolutely. Once a senator gets involved, everything becomes a totally different ball game. It's turning into a complete circus."

"Look, all I want to do is get this over with. Get the spotlight off Lucy. Is there any way we can do that?"

"Well, there are really two questions. One is how someone got access to the email system so they could spoof the sender names and send stuff to a private email list. The other question is how someone got access to the electronic health record so they could pull out everybody's psychiatric medications."

"Can you guys help us figure out how they did it?"

"We could. This is the kind of thing the health system hired us to do. I'm putting Michael to work on it. We'll get some preliminary data, and then we'll talk to the health system and see if they want us to do more."

Michael was a really smart MIT classmate of ours who now worked for Yuri.

"The senator thing sort of scares me," I said.

"I agree. If the feds come in and start clamping down on this, it could slow any investigation down to a snail's pace. You get the federal government involved and we'll probably need to have ten people sign off on everything we do."

"And do you think this relates at all to the murder?"

"That's the question, isn't it?"

Yuri started bouncing super high.

"I've got it!" Yuri was like that. He'd suddenly get hit by these brainstorm bolts of lightning that came zinging in from left field.

"We rattle cages," he said with a gleeful smile.

"Rattle cages? That's your big idea?"

"Right. We'll do the obvious too, of course. We'll gather data. We'll correlate data. We'll mine data. All that stuff. But especially with the senator hanging around, that could take a long time."

"A snail's pace."

"Exactly. Although it's really worse than that. With a US senator messing everything up, the federal government might wind up making a snail look like a bunny rabbit."

Great. Terrific.

"So, instead we rattle cages, huh? How do we do that?" I asked.

"We let people know that very sophisticated people are working really hard to solve this thing."

"And that will rattle their cage?"

"Exactly. For sure. We try to really scare the crap out of whoever did this. Flush them out and see what happens. IntelliSciTech will start looking into the technical aspects of this. In the meantime, see if you can figure out how we can rattle some cages."

"That's my assignment?"

"Exactly. What do you think?"

The obvious person was Vikram. But I wasn't sure what we could do to rattle Vikram's cage. "Yuri, you have to give me more to work with than that."

"Look, it's not the Chinese government doing this. It's not a nation-state. This is some smart but seriously twisted individual. Or maybe a couple of smart, twisted individuals working together. That's all this is."

"Thanks, Yuri. I'll think about it." His enthusiasm was infectious, but I really didn't know where to start. I thought about what he had said. My assignment was to figure out how to rattle Vikram's cage.

"You think whoever sent those emails is really smart?" I asked.

"Smart? Yes. Probably."

"Smarter than you guys?"

Yuri shrugged. "Gideon, don't worry about it. It doesn't matter. He can't have anything like our resources. IntelliSciTech may not be a nation-state, but we're pretty much the next closest thing."

"And you can bring those resources to bear?"

"I don't care what the health system actually pays us. If we need to do it, it will be done." Yuri smiled. "We'll do it for you, Gideon."

He was really bouncing away at this point.

I now apparently had the closest thing to a nation-state behind me. I wasn't sure exactly what that meant, but it sounded scary—scary for the other guy, that is.

Good for me.

24

I thought hard about what to do about Vikram. I decided that there was absolutely nothing to be gained by talking to him myself. I had no leverage and he'd just clam up. Then he'd make absolutely sure that any possible evidence pointing to him was destroyed. I suppose I might have contacted the police or the hospital lawyers and told them what I'd found out. But the more I thought about that, the more convinced I was that it would be a waste of time.

I realized there was absolutely no way that I personally could rattle Vikram's cage. But then I had a brain flash. I realized how I could rattle Vikram's cage really hard, and he wouldn't even know it was me.

So, I activated Plan Z.

That's what I was calling it. Plan Z involved contacting Gwen Swann and arranging another covert meeting in the parking garage. We met late that afternoon in the same place and once again kept our cars about twenty yards apart. I was getting much more comfortable with this *sub rosa* business. But I knew I couldn't drop my guard. I arrived twenty minutes early and watched every car that came into the parking garage very carefully.

As I climbed into the passenger seat of Gwen's car, I smiled.

"This is Plan Z," I informed her.

"Plan Z, huh," she said. "What happened to plans A, B, C, D, and all the rest of them?"

"None of them were going to work."

"OK, Plan Z. Tell me more."

I told her all about Namrata and Vikram. How I'd done the Google searches and found their engagement announcement. How I'd talked to Rachael Ward. And why I was now convinced that Vikram had sent the emails. I gave her the printout of the engagement announcement and of the Google search that found it. I also gave her a copy of my list of search terms.

"You should do this same search, and also try some other searches using different combinations of these terms. Just so you see how it works," I said. "Then print out your own copy of these, and make sure you shred mine. Can you do that?"

She smiled. "No problem at all. We're very good at shredding paper. We have a special machine that grinds everything up into tiny pieces, mixes them with water, and turns it all into paste."

"That's awesome. I'd love to see it work." I wondered how much those machines cost. Probably a lot.

"So, let's hear about Plan Z," she said.

"It's an assignment, really. The heart of Plan Z involves you doing me a big favor."

"That's fine. Like I said, Gideon, I am happy to help. I have to say, though, that we don't have enough yet to publish anything about Vikram. If you want me to publish something, you need to get me more."

"That's fine. I don't need you to publish anything. But if we did want to publish something, what would you need?"

"We'd need something really concrete that linked Vikram to the emails, maybe some kind of highly technical analysis that proved the email came from his computer. Actually, it doesn't have to be highly technical. It could be something simple. But it would need to be persuasive. Ideally, some expert should be able to say conclusively that the email came from Vikram."

"But this stuff I just gave you is still useful, right? It's the kind of thing you want?"

"Oh definitely. It's great. There is a story here. We just need more before we publish anything."

"And without this material, you'd know nothing about it."

"That's how investigative reporting works. I get some leads.

I follow up on those leads. I just keep putting one foot in front of the other. With a little hard work and a bit of luck, we get enough to write a story we can publish."

"Good. Plan Z may actually help. But Plan Z is a little bit proactive."

"A little bit proactive, huh, Gideon?"

"Yeah, maybe just a tiny little pinch of proactivity."

"And I'll bet you want me to do the *proaction*," she said, "if that's the correct term."

"Yes, please," I said. "That's the favor."

"What do I do? This tiny little pinch of proactivity."

"I want you to call Vikram. Tell him you are writing a story about the emails. Tell him you would like to talk to him. But I really don't care what he says. It's fine if he says nothing at all. The real goal is to really rattle his cage with your phone call. I want to give Vikram's cage a hard shake."

"What are you suggesting that I say?"

"Well, first of all make sure he knows about the story you just published about the merger and the takeover. That way he knows you're credible."

"I can do that. But why shouldn't I try to get information out of him?"

"I really doubt he'll say much. But use your judgment. Like I said, though, that's not the point. The goal of Plan Z is to light a little fire under Vikram. To make him think that everything he has done is about to come spilling out and will soon be splashed all over the media."

"Actually, this is not a bad concept. He'll have no idea how much I might or might not know."

"Tell him you know all about the engagement. Maybe read him a few lines from the announcement. He may not even know about that yet. It was posted by his parents in India and that was only last week. But much more important, tell him you've heard that IntelliSciTech Systems has been hired by the health system to investigate the emails."

IntelliSciTech Systems was the key ingredient of Plan Z.

"How do you spell it?" she asked.

I wrote it down for her.

"Have they been hired?"

"They are already helping the health system with cybersecurity. They are just starting to look into the emails. I can give you the name of someone who works there who can confirm this. But you have to keep anything he tells you as background. He can confirm what I'm telling you."

I gave her the main number at IntelliSciTech as well as Yuri's name and extension. I figured she would want to know she was actually talking to someone who worked there. I had called Yuri and he said this was OK. After all, it was his idea to rattle people's cages, and this would do that for sure.

"Yuri's expecting your call. He is head of one of their major divisions."

"What exactly is IntelliSciTech Systems?"

"It's a huge company that focuses on cybersecurity. How to create it and how to penetrate it. Most of what they do, nobody has the vaguest clue. A lot of it is subcontracted from the intelligence community."

"Vikram will know about them?"

"It is hard to imagine that Vikram doesn't know about them. But if he doesn't, he can find out easily enough. It's all over the internet and it's really quite scary. It will freak him out."

"Why so? I mean specifically, in what way?"

"They have access to all sorts of very advanced tools. Highly secret tools. Network analysis tools. Things like that. In fact, they build malware for cyber warfare. I know that because some friends of mine from school work for them. They never really say anything, but you can figure it out."

Gwen jotted all this down. When she got to "cyber warfare," she added two exclamation points.

"IntelliSciTech," I continued, "can pick things out of network routers that even the router designers don't know are there. Tiny little digital footprints left by network traffic. Plus, they can download whatever is stored on a PC and reconstruct everything that's been recently deleted. That's actually very easy. And if they really want to, I'll bet they can take any encrypted file, send it off to some huge cluster somewhere, and eventually break the code."

"You're sure Vikram will know all this?" Gwen asked.

"Vikram has a PhD in computer science from IIT Bangalore. That means he's smart enough and sophisticated enough that the very thought of IntelliSciTech will scare the crap out of him. That's the beauty of Plan Z."

"How long would it take for them to get started?" She read the name from her notes. "IntelliSciTech Systems, I mean."

"No time at all. They don't have to be there physically. They'd just come in over the network. And since they're already hired, they could already have copied all sorts of data out onto their machines. They could have moved it all to secret clusters tucked away all around the country. They could be analyzing it as we speak."

"What would they do?"

"I have no idea. But they could pick apart Laurel Hill Hospital's network and all the computers attached to it in ways that none of us could even imagine. Vikram would have to assume that once they get in there, everything that he has been doing will suddenly become transparent. *Everything!* He may be smart, but these guys are way smarter. And they have access to resources that are, for all practical purposes, unlimited."

"And you're sure he'll know this."

"Vikram will quickly figure all this out."

"OK, so let me make sure I understand what you are trying to do. You want Vikram to believe that everything he has been doing is about to be blasted totally out into the open. That I know all about his relationship with Namrata. That I have discovered his engagement announcement. And we particularly want him to know that IntelliSciTech is coming in to find out what's going on. That they are coming in very fast and very hard."

I wasn't sure where she got that from, but I loved it.

"In fact," she continued, "they are probably already there. And on top of all that, *The Boston World* is about to put all this stuff right out there on our front page."

"You got it. What do you think?"

"I think if I give him a phone call and communicate all that to him, Vikram will totally crap in his pants. On the spot."

"So, you'll do it?"

"Gideon, you need to tell me what this is all about. Why are you asking me to do this? What's the point?"

I told her about the senator and how the federal government was getting involved in the investigation. I told her how all that would make a snail look like a bunny rabbit. Any official investigation would likely take forever. But Vikram wouldn't know any of that.

I told her that I had decided that the only way to push forward quickly was to rattle Vikram's cage really hard. I didn't mention that it was Yuri's idea. She seemed to get the concept.

"This should generate news and you'll have the inside track," I said.

She nodded.

"So, you'll do it?" I asked again.

"You bet. I'll do it. This is good. Of course, first I have to call this Yuri person and get confirmation. I'll also get as much information about Yuri as I can. I have to believe what he's telling me."

"Yuri is very well known. I don't think you'll have any problem there."

"Good."

"When do you think you'll call him? Vikram, I mean," I asked.

"Not today. I need to think this all through. I need to script the call. I need to know exactly what I want to say, and how I want to handle various things Vikram might say."

I nodded.

"I'll definitely call him sometime tomorrow morning," she said. "I suspect that the best way to do this will be to be very matter-of-fact. Very down to earth. I'll concentrate on sounding very professional and let the content of what I'm saying do all the work."

"Great. In the meantime, I am working on something else that's very interesting. Something that is connected to all this but very different."

"What's that?"

"It's too early to talk about it, but I can give you a hint. Two words."

"Two words?"

"Cardiac surgery."

"Cardiac surgery? Gideon, what the heck does cardiac surgery have to do with any of this?"

"I'm still working on that. I'll give you a call in a couple of days. In the meantime, let's see if you can maybe get Vikram to explode."

"I'll be lighting the fuse tomorrow morning."

OK!

Plan Z was off the launchpad and accelerating into orbit. Hopefully it would reach warp speed sometime around midday tomorrow.

25

Rachael Ward's office was in an eight-story wing of Laurel Hill Hospital that was fifty yards or so from the much larger ten-story wing that held all the clinical floors and the ORs. The two wings were connected on the first two floors by an atrium that served as the main entrance to the hospital. The top two floors of Rachael's wing housed the executive offices. Rachael was on the fifth floor. Even so, her windows provided an impressive view of the extended suburbs of Boston.

I wanted to talk to Rachael, but I felt much more comfortable just stopping by and hoping to catch her in rather than calling and trying to make an appointment. She was at her desk, engrossed in something that required looking back and forth between two monitors. I knocked gently.

"Hi, Rachael," I said, trying not to startle her. "I stopped by to see if you had found out anything more."

"You mean about the angiograms?" she asked.

"You told me a group of consultants was analyzing the cardiac image database and that they might know something by now."

"You're right. They do. They were here this morning for about two hours."

"What did they say?"

"They said a whole lot. And they gave me this big fat report." She held up a bound document. "It's a hundred and forty pages and it's very technical. Lots of tables. Lots of details. But the overall concept is really pretty simple."

The hefty report presumably reflected a desire to charge the hospital a hefty fee.

"Can I look at it?" I asked.

"Sure."

She handed it to me. It looked very professional. I scanned the table of contents and the executive summary.

"Like I said," she continued, "the basic concept is simple. The database of angiogram images is all messed up. It looks like someone made one set of changes and then tried to change it all back. Or maybe somebody else tried to change it back. But didn't do it right."

"Can they tell what the first set of changes were?" I asked.

"It looks like someone started off with maybe forty angiogram images that showed different types of coronary artery disease. Major blockages in different coronary arteries. Things like that." She was looking at the executive summary at the beginning of the report.

"OK."

"Then it looks like they went through two or three years of angiogram data for lots of different patients. They must have looked at the written notes in each patient's record and then substituted one of the forty angiogram images for whatever image was actually there. But they only did this for less than half the patients."

"If they did that, there must be copies of each phony image in several patient records. Duplicates."

She flipped through the report and opened it to one of the appendices.

"Exactly," she said, looking at a table. "There are maybe ten or twenty copies of each phony image. Sometimes more."

"But isn't there patient data in each of the image files? Things like the patient's name, the patient's hospital ID, the date the study was done? Things like that?"

"That was all changed. When they substituted one of the image files, they somehow changed all that data so that it matched the patient record it was attached to."

"So, this was some kind of cover-up?"

"We think they were putting images that showed significant disease into records of patients who basically had pretty healthy hearts, according to the actual angiogram images they replaced."

"That sounds stupid. Why would anyone do that?" I asked.

"Well, a year and a half ago an audit team came through to evaluate cardiac surgery at Laurel Hill."

"They suspected something?"

"No. Not at all. Heart surgery here is highly regarded. They were thinking they might really ramp up our program here. Nobody thought we were doing anything wrong."

"And the audit team didn't find out about any of this."

"We passed with flying colors. I don't know what the evaluators actually looked at, but they went away extremely impressed. Their report said the program was great and that we had tremendous potential for growth. Who knows if they even looked at the angiograms?"

"And then after they left, someone tried to put everything back the way it was."

"Apparently. And it appears that they didn't have a very good programmer doing that part of it. They must have had someone pretty good doing the first set of changes."

She pulled out a manila folder and opened it.

"Here, let me show you."

She sat down at a small table and arranged several pieces of paper in front of her. "See, here is one of the original angiogram images, and here is the phony one they replaced it with."

I pulled a chair over to sit kitty-corner to her at the table. She twisted the images forty-five degrees so we could both look at them easily.

As I pulled up my chair and started looking at the two images, the sides of our knees touched momentarily under the table.

It was one of those odd experiences.

All I could think was, *Hey, that feels sort of nice.*

Normally, I would have moved my leg away without any particular thought as soon as something like that happened. But I guess I was startled and distracted by the physical contact with Rachael.

In the approximately one half second that I sat there thinking about this, Rachael moved her knee away. And continued to talk about the two images.

I should have moved my knee. I felt like a dirty old man.

We continued our examination of the images. I started out looking for small areas where the coronary arteries were blocked. But then I suddenly realized that wasn't the point at all.

"These are completely different hearts," I said.

I was of course stating the obvious. This was what she had been telling me, but it didn't fully register until I looked at the images themselves. The pattern of all the arteries was different. It was like looking at the maps of two different river deltas that were very similar but different in the fine detail.

"Exactly," she said, "but both images have the same patient name, the same ID, and the same date when the imaging study was supposedly performed."

"So, all the original images are also still there? In the database."

"The images are all in a big file system. And all of them are still there—all the real ones and all the phony ones. The patient records were changed to point at the phony images. Then it appears that somebody tried to change it so that they pointed at the correct images, but messed it all up instead."

"But everything is still there?"

"Yes. If they had changed all the pointers back correctly and then deleted all the phony copies, nobody would ever have known about the switch."

"You know, it's sort of funny that Arnold was the person who discovered this."

"Yes, of all people," Rachael agreed. "You're right."

"You think this is a motive for murder?"

This was the eight-hundred-pound gorilla in the room as far as I was concerned.

"I think people have been killed for a lot less," she said.

I nodded. That was the truth.

"What happens now?" I asked.

"You got me. I don't really know what to do. What do you think, Gideon? I need to tell somebody about all this, but I'm not sure who."

"Who hired the consultants?"

"I hired them. Dr. Arnold told me to. They report back to me."

"Do any of Arnold's staff know anything about this?"

"I think so, but I don't know who."

"What do you really think? Do you think this might have been why Arnold was killed? To cover this up?"

"It's possible." She shook her head. "Without the consultants and without this report, this whole issue would have just died right here with Dr. Arnold gone."

I tried to get my mind around this. From a completely selfish perspective, the only thing that really mattered to me was Lucy.

"Do you have any idea who else might know about this?"

"Dr. Arnold was keeping this whole thing super secret until he could find out what was going on. Whoever he talked to about it, he kept to himself."

"If someone killed him, do you think they might try to kill you?"

And maybe kill me too, for that matter, now that I know about it.

"If somebody is trying to cover this up and Dr. Arnold told them about me, I guess they might. I mean, if they killed once, is it that big a deal to kill again? . . . I think I have to be careful who I talk to about it."

"I agree," I said, "but I think you do need to tell somebody."

"But who, Gideon? I mean who specifically? I can't take this to the Laurel Hill cardiac surgeons, that's for sure. Someone there must have switched the images. Should I go to Larry Bryant?"

Larry Bryant had taken over from Arnold as acting CEO of the health system.

"But that somehow doesn't feel right either," she continued. "This is really about Laurel Hill Hospital, not the health system."

It suddenly occurred to me that maybe I could kill two birds with one stone if I put her in touch with Ebenezer Clarke, Laurel Hill's kid lawyer. That would solve her problem. And it would maybe make him think that I was bowing out of all this, and dutifully turning it all over to him. And he would definitely know who else to talk to. Laurel Hill would probably want to keep this under wraps until they figured out what was really going on.

"I have a suggestion," I said. "I was recently talking to Ben Clarke. He is one of the lawyers who works for Laurel Hill. He's in their risk management office."

"He's new. I haven't met him yet. You think I should talk to him?"

"Yes, I do."

"Do you know him well?"

"Well enough. I was talking to him just last week."

"I think I would feel funny leaving a message about this with some secretary," she said.

I pulled out the card that Ben had given me and showed it to her along with the cell phone number he wrote on the back.

"That's his cell phone. Want me to call it?"

"Please. I'd really appreciate that."

I dialed the number. It rang five times and switched over to voicemail.

"Hello, Ben. This is Gideon. Gideon Lowell. You gave me your cell number and told me to call you anytime. I have a fairly urgent question. Could you call me back?" I gave him my cell number.

I hung up and looked at Rachael.

"How's that?"

"That's great. Nobody can connect me to that at all."

"When he calls back, I'll just tell him I have someone he needs to talk to. Then I'll bring him here and introduce you to him. That way nobody sees you going to his office. And nobody knows anything until you meet him in person. Even Ben won't know what this is all about until he meets you."

"That's great. Just call me on my cell and I'll make sure I'm here. This obviously takes complete priority."

"OK, it's a plan. If he doesn't call soon, I'll go over to his office and see what's going on."

"What do you think he'll do?"

"I have no idea. He's a lawyer. They have their own take on things. We'll see."

I remembered how Ben had described his role. *Protect the*

hospital was what it boiled down to. As I thought about that, I had a sinking feeling that he might try to hush up the whole thing.

I didn't think I wanted that to happen. As far as I was concerned, the best way to help Lucy was to get everything out in the open as quickly as possible. If young Ebenezer tried to keep this confidential, I'd have to figure out how I could jerk his legs out from under him.

In a completely *sub rosa* fashion, of course.

26

"Now that I know more about you, Gideon, I am beginning to wonder whether it's your pirate ancestry I need to worry about, not your political connections."

Glenn Santoro, the Boston police detective, had called and told me he wanted to talk. So we agreed to meet at my office at Boston Central Hospital in the Department of Emergency Medicine.

I wondered what Santoro thought of the somewhat decrepit building they had put us in. Boston Central was a conglomeration of connected buildings built over the course of many decades. Because the floors of the various buildings were at slightly different levels, you often found yourself going up and down small stairways as you went from one building to another.

The patient care areas were state of the art. Since none of the faculty in the emergency medicine department actually saw patients in our offices, we got stuck in an old building that really needed a lot of work. Renovating it didn't seem to be anyone's priority.

Santoro was smiling at me as usual. I continued to get the feeling that I amused him. But then, everything seemed to amuse him.

"My pirate ancestry?" I asked. I was not sure what he was getting at.

"Yes. Your pirate ancestry. Apparently, you got kicked out of MIT."

"That's not true."

"No?"

"I did withdraw. Is that what you mean? That was the spring semester of my sophomore year. I withdrew voluntarily. I returned the next semester. You can check my transcript."

"I did look at your transcript. I have it right here." He pulled a few pages out of a folder he was holding. "In fact, I also have the transcripts of four other MIT students," he continued, "four of your classmates. They all apparently withdrew on the exact same day that you did, and the explanation on their transcripts is verbatim identical to yours."

How did Santoro ever get those transcripts? Maybe schools gave them to the police if they asked. But how did Santoro even know to ask? I knew what was coming next, but I decided to play it simpleminded.

"Yes. That's correct," I said. "Five of us withdrew at the same time."

"And I also notice that all five of you had taken the same course the previous fall—Advanced System Programming I. Three of you got A+s. The other two got As. You were one of the A+s, Gideon. Why am I not surprised?"

It sounded like the cat was out of the bag. Even so, I wasn't about to volunteer any information. I'd wait and see where this was going.

"It was a fun course," I said.

"And all five of you were enrolled in Advanced Systems Programming II in the spring when you all got kicked out."

"Withdrew," I corrected him.

"OK. I agree. You officially withdrew. But why do I think you all basically got kicked out?" He laughed mockingly.

"You know," I said, "I really can't talk about that. We are supposed to refer all questions about that to the MIT Office of Student Affairs."

"Well, Gideon, I could call MIT—maybe call their office of student affairs, that's a good idea—and ask for their formal permission to interrogate you in the course of an ongoing murder investigation."

The more I saw of Santoro, the more I was reminded of the actor

Peter Falk's portrayal of the bumbling detective Columbo. People always underestimated Columbo and wound up getting nailed.

Santoro was not bumbling, but he had this friendly, mildly amused approach to the world. And I thought the world really did amuse him. But I suspected that he played that fact up consciously, or maybe subconsciously. And it probably made people drop their guard.

I had to avoid that trap. He was definitely not my friend.

In any case, it hardly seemed worth fighting him on what he already knew.

"What do you want from me, Detective?"

"Maybe you could tell me what all this was about." He held up the five transcripts with a little flourish, like he was signaling a waiter or maybe politely hailing a taxi cab.

"Well, all five of us did a term project together for the fall course. The professor, his name was John O'Brien, did research on operating system security. His graduate students had built a system that was supposed to be super secure. Impregnable."

"I gather it wasn't."

"Our term project was to try to break into it. O'Brien didn't think we could do it, but he wanted to see what interesting ideas we could come up with to try."

"What happened?"

"We took that stupid system completely apart. We found six distinct ways to break into it. O'Brien's graduate students were humiliated. One of them had to completely redo his entire PhD thesis and wound up spending an extra two years in graduate school."

"But that didn't get you kicked out?"

"Not at all. O'Brien was ecstatic. We all got an A+ for the project."

"So, why did you get kicked out?"

"Well, O'Brien had contracts with a bank and with an aerospace company to test their cybersecurity. So, he gave us that as our term project for the spring semester."

"And you succeeded?"

"Absolutely. First we built a bunch of tools based on what we had done in the fall. Then we used the tools. We broke into both systems pretty easily."

"And that got you kicked out?"

"No, that was fine."

"What then?"

"Well, someone, I don't know who, took those tools and broke into a couple of other banks, into several of MIT's administrative systems, and into a CIA database. Maybe other places too. I don't know. Whoever did it was just trying to show people that everything was very insecure. That was all. He thought people would be happy to find out. He didn't steal anything or anything like that."

"This was someone on your student project team who did this?"

"Yes, one of us must have done it, maybe more than one. But definitely not me. And I don't know who it was." He probably didn't believe this, but he was clearly smart enough to know that I was going to stick to that story no matter what.

"What happened?"

"Well, as you might expect, MIT went nuts. But none of the targets wanted anything to get out about any of it. And MIT was incredibly embarrassed. MIT's name was written all over the whole thing. After all, this was MIT students working for an MIT professor on a term project for an MIT course. And it's a really famous course. That course has a real reputation."

"A reputation?"

"As a ball-buster. When you apply for a job in computers, industry looks specifically at how you did in that course."

"So, MIT hushed it up."

"Yes. They hushed it up. But they felt they had to do something. And none of us would tell them who actually did it. So, they gave us a choice. Voluntarily withdraw or else they would think up something much less pleasant for us. One way or another we'd be out. So, we withdrew."

"So, you're not just a doctor? All this computer stuff is not a big mystery to you?"

"I didn't have anything to do with sending those emails, if that's what you mean."

"But you might know enough to try to investigate those emails."

"Why would I do that? I don't think anybody seriously thinks I sent that email—the one that supposedly came from me. I talked to Boston Central's IT after I found out about it. They seemed to know what to do. And they completely understood that I didn't send it."

"What about Yuri Marin? You think he might have done it?"

Yuri had been one of my project teammates who had been forced to withdraw from MIT at the same time.

"Do what? Send the email? No way. Why in the world would he do that? What does Yuri have to do with this?"

I was getting worried. It sounded like another cat was about to get loose from another bag.

"I meant breaking into all those systems back when you were at MIT."

"Like I told you. Nobody knows who did it. All I know is I didn't have anything to do with that."

"I was speaking to Yuri earlier today," Santoro said. "He tells me you said you want him to investigate those emails."

"He told you that?"

"Yes. He told me that."

"No, he didn't." I looked at him for a moment and our eyes locked. "Well, maybe Yuri said something like that. But he didn't say that."

"How so?" Santoro smirked. He was clearly having fun watching me squirm.

"Yuri works for IntelliSciTech Systems. Boston Central hired IntelliSciTech to help with their cybersecurity. Yuri is in overall charge of one of the major divisions working on that kind of stuff."

"But you did talk to him?"

"Yuri is a good friend."

"You talked to him recently about those emails?"

"Yes, but it was his suggestion that his group might look into it. He's going to talk to Boston Central about it."

"We have two emails connected to an ongoing murder investigation. And we have two computer hackers who got kicked out of MIT for maybe breaking into a CIA database running around doing something that looks like investigating. Is that what you're telling me?"

"No. I am not telling you anything like that. I'm not involved. If Yuri does anything, it will be because Boston Central Health System is paying him to do it. And if he does get involved in all this, that's a good thing. Believe me, the Boston Police Department does not have anyone even remotely as sophisticated as Yuri. You should be happy if he winds up working on this."

Santoro's reaction to this assertion was completely unreadable.

"So where are the other three guys?"

"One works with Yuri at IntelliSciTech. The other two are down at a place called Liberty Crossing in Virginia."

"Oh, terrific. So now you're saying that there are actually three of you guys sniffing around this investigation. Is that what you're telling me?"

"Seriously, all I want is to get the spotlight off Lucy. Get this whole thing over with, so we can get on with our lives. That's all I want."

He glared at me, perhaps mapping his next move.

"I'm trying to decide how tricky you really are." He looked at me for a moment longer and then leaned back and smiled.

"I don't know what to say." I smiled back at him.

Santoro was cagey.

"Tell me something more about this pirate ancestry of yours," he said. "What did Captain Gideon the pirate actually do? Did he make people walk the plank?"

"I can't imagine he ever did anything like that. I think he just pulled his ship up next to theirs and politely relieved them of their cargo."

"A gentleman pirate. Kind of like you, huh?"

"If he was alive today, he'd probably be working on Wall Street."

"With a big home in the Hamptons, maybe?"

"Yeah. That too. I guess that's today's equivalent of a pirate island in the Caribbean."

"I've never been to the Hamptons," Santoro said, "so I really have no idea."

"I've never been there either."

We talked a bit more, and then as he was leaving, he switched back into his cop persona.

"You know I've got my eye on you." He looked me directly in the eyes and pointed at my face. "Take my advice and stay out of this case."

I had this sudden urge to wink at him and say, "Catch me if you can!"

But I'd gotten pretty good at suppressing urges like that.

"All I want to do is get the spotlight off Lucy," I repeated.

I really needed to stay on message at all times.

27

Lucy cheerfully greeted me as I walked in the door.

"Hi, Gideon. Guess what. The saga of Namrata continues to unfold."

Something good must have happened.

We went into the kitchen. The kids were watching TV in the living room. They officially got an hour a day, but they got half an hour more if they watched it all in Spanish, which they usually did. Lucy flipped back and forth between Spanish and English when she talked to them at home. They were much more fluent than me.

I could smell dinner cooking on the stove.

"What's going on?"

"Namrata is in India," she said.

India? This was certainly not what I expected to hear.

"How do you know that?"

"She called Strier. She apparently left in a complete rush. Without doing anything ahead of time. She didn't tell anybody. Of course, she was off the OR schedule, but she's still being paid, so she's supposed to show up. I thought she was going to resign. She just left."

"What did she say to Strier when she called?"

"She said she wants to resign. She was asking him how to do it."

"From India?"

"From India."

"Did she say anything else?"

"Yes actually, she did. She said she's getting married."

This was getting more and more interesting.

"Did she say to whom?"

"I have no idea. But Strier got the idea that the wedding's going to happen pretty soon. And she did say she'll be staying permanently in India."

"So she just upped and left," I said. "Suddenly. To get married. That doesn't sound normal." It sounded like there must be something else going on. I was pretty sure I knew what that was.

"I agree. But I think Indians do marriage differently than we do." Lucy shrugged, and then continued. "Oh, and another thing I heard from one of the staff. All of her stuff is still here in her apartment. She left it all behind. None of it's packed or anything. She's going to pay someone to clear it out. They'll ship some of it to India and dispose of the rest. She took a couple of suitcases with her on the plane, but that's all. Strange, huh?"

Definitely strange. But definitely very good.

"Well, I guess that takes care of Namrata," I said.

"It sure does. Boy, what a relief. I can't believe she's not going to be around anymore. It was like magic. Suddenly, *poof,* she's gone."

I liked the image. And I was virtually certain that Vikram disappeared in the very same *poof.*

"Do you know when she left?" I asked.

"Apparently the plane left Logan the day before yesterday in the evening. She got into Delhi early in the morning today. She probably changed planes somewhere."

That meant that Namrata had left the very evening of the day that Gwen called Vikram to rattle his cage. This was a lot more than just rattling a cage. This was picking the cage up, shaking it really hard, turning it upside down, and watching Vikram free-fall out the bottom. This was great.

This was absolutely spectacular.

In fact, the more I thought about it, the more certain I was that this was exactly what happened. Vikram had panicked and fled to India, taking his bride-to-be with him.

I was very curious to know if this was indeed what happened. But I knew I couldn't ask. I had to lay low. I'd find out soon enough.

Lucy looked at me and shook her head, as if to clear it. "Wow," she said.

That pretty much summed it up.

Of course, this didn't solve the basic problem. We still didn't know who murdered Arnold. But now at least Namrata was totally out of the picture. In fact, Namrata was now permanently on the other side of the planet. And Vikram had been flushed out of hiding.

With Yuri's help behind the scenes, I was pretty sure we could now pin the emails on Vikram. Even if we couldn't absolutely prove it, we could make pretty clear to everybody what had happened. And even more important, it was already done. *Poof.* We didn't have to wait while the US government slowed everything to a glacial pace.

"Wow is right," I said.

It felt like a lot of progress.

But we were actually no closer to our ultimate goal.

28

Gwen and I were *sub rosa* again in the parking garage. This time it was early afternoon and was very hot outside. Sweltering. Gwen kept her car engine on with the air conditioner running.

"Hi, Gwen," I said. "I have decided that you have a magic wand."

"I have a magic wand?"

"You waved it at Vikram and suddenly, *poof*, he disappeared."

"He sure did, didn't he?"

"He decamped to the other side of the planet."

"I still have to figure out how to write that up."

We sat watching shoppers walk back and forth between the garage and the mall as we talked about Vikram. Then I sprang my next idea.

"I'd like to get you started thinking about something."

"Is this about cardiac surgery? Like you mentioned the last time we met?"

"Yes, that's it exactly. How would you like to start doing some research on cardiac surgery? Specifically, about unnecessary coronary artery bypass surgery. I think that is where this whole thing is going next, and I think you could write some very interesting stories about it. General articles, too. Not just stories about this case."

"But linked to this case?"

"Yes, absolutely. Linked directly to this case."

"So what's the deal with cardiac surgery?"

"Let's do this. Let's pretend that I'm a cardiologist and that you are a fifty-five-year-old man with chest pain."

"OK."

"Good, so tell me about your problem. What brings you in to see me today?"

Gwen thought for a moment, getting mentally into the role. I could see her saying OK to herself. Then she spoke to me, the cardiologist.

"Doc, I got chest pain," she said. "I am afraid I'm going to have a heart attack." She looked over at me. "You mean something like that?"

"Yeah. I ask you about the pain and see if it sounds like cardiac pain."

"OK."

"So, does it come on when you exert yourself?"

I nodded, so she said, "Yes."

"Can you take your finger and point to exactly where the pain is?"

This time I shook my head and got a "No."

"Does it radiate to your left shoulder?"

A nod from me and a yes from her.

"And does it have a sort of crushing quality, like maybe a baby elephant is sitting on your chest?"

"Yes, exactly like a baby elephant, Doc, how did you know?" Gwen was getting into the swing of things.

"And does it go away when you sit down and rest?"

"Yeah. That's exactly it. So what do you think? Am I gonna die?"

"I hope not," I said, "but first things first. We need to figure out what's going on. So first I schedule you for a stress test. Let's pretend I do this and it's positive. That means your heart muscle is not getting all the blood it needs to function properly. And that's why you have the chest pain."

"OK."

"Then the next step is a cardiac angiogram," I said. "To do this, I inject dye into the little vessels that supply blood to your heart muscle itself. They're called coronary arteries. I take a video while I'm doing this. I'm looking for places where the coronary arteries are blocked. Sometimes I can fix a blockage right away by inserting a small expandable tube called a stent. OK?"

"OK."

"Well, your angiogram shows several critical blockages, but unfortunately I can't fix any of them with a stent. So, I am sending you to a cardiac surgeon. He will look at the video and see where he might be able to sew in little veins to bypass those blockages and let the blood flow smoothly."

"Fine, bring him on."

"But now let's pretend that you, Gwen, are the cardiac surgeon and I am the patient."

"Oh, good." Gwen seemed happy to no longer be the patient. She thought for a moment. "And I want you to know," she continued, "that I've had a lot of experience doing these procedures. If anyone can save your life, it's me."

"That's extremely reassuring, Gwen," I said. "So now, you're talking to me and trying to decide what to do next. I am sitting there in your office. If you decide I do not need bypass surgery, you can tell me to go back to my cardiologist and he will put me on medicine. If you do this, you get paid two hundred dollars. I'm making these numbers up."

"But if I decide you need me to operate?"

"Then you get paid twenty-five thousand. So, what do you think we should do?"

"Hmm. Let me think now. Send you away and collect two hundred bucks, or operate and collect twenty-five grand. Hmm. Well, my wife really wants a new car."

"Gwen, I am so very proud of you. You are picking up the subtleties of clinical medicine very quickly."

"No, seriously, how do you decide? There must be degrees of severity and things like that."

"Yes, of course. So, let's pretend that there is a little scale, like a gas gauge with a little arrow that can swing from one to ten. And let's pretend that if it shows nine or ten, everyone would agree that you need surgery. And if it is seven or eight, most people would agree. And if it is four or less, people agree that surgery is not needed."

"Five and six is a gray area?"

"Right."

"If it is five or six, there is a huge incentive for me personally to just go ahead and operate."

"Yup. Your wife gets her car."

"So, the incentives are screwed up. Is that what you're telling me?"

"That's American medicine. And yes, that is part of what I'm saying. Unfortunately, that's what fee-for-service medicine is all about. If this was England where they have nationalized medicine, the severity would need to be eight or higher to operate. Of course, I'm just making up this scale to make it easy to understand. There is no scale like this. Or maybe there is; I really don't know."

Gwen was nodding and scribbling down notes.

"There is one more question I want to ask you," I said.

"Shoot."

"What if I am in the range of one to four on the scale? What do you do then?"

"Well, I shouldn't operate. You said everybody agrees about that."

"I didn't ask what *should* you do. I asked what *will* you do. Remember, I am sitting there in front of you in your office, and you have to decide what to do."

"You're saying that some surgeons will operate anyway?"

"I am wondering how many might operate anyway. I really don't know. That why I'm asking you to research it. See what you can find about unnecessary coronary bypass surgery."

"And this relates to something that is going on at Laurel Hill?"

"I think there is a very good chance that it does."

"I thought Laurel Hill had a really good cardiac surgery program."

"It has a very good reputation. It has very good outcomes. But there are two ways to have good outcomes. Guess what they are?"

"You tell me. Gideon, you're starting to scare me."

"One way is to do good surgery and provide good postoperative care."

"And the second way?"

"Always operate on patients who have healthy hearts in the first place."

"Oh no. God. Gideon, this is really great stuff."

"I thought you said it was scary."

"Gideon, honestly, the scarier the better. The paper loves scary. People pay money to read about scary."

"So, you'll look into this?"

"I'll have a couple of staff start working on this right away."

"OK, you might start with a PubMed search. You'll find a whole lot of articles talking about whether coronary bypass surgery is worthwhile in the first place. That is not what I am talking about. As far as I am concerned, a huge number of people have been helped by coronary bypass surgery. The real question is how many patients get it who don't really need it. But have your researchers read about all of this. If you wind up wanting to write a more general article, you'll probably want to talk about the whole thing."

"That's fine. We'll cast the net widely."

"But please don't publish anything yet. Right now, this is background."

"You tell me when it's time. I assume that will be soon. I gather you need more information to link it to the case?"

"Yes, but it's more than that. I think you may be able to help break this one wide open too. Light a little fire under people and make them explode. Just like we did with Vikram. Like you did, I mean."

"I just did what you told me."

"Right. With your magic wand. You wave it at people, and they go *poof*. At least that's the concept. Like with Vikram."

"OK, fine. My magic wand. Keep it coming."

29

What was the point of having the next best thing to a nation-state backing you up if you never used it? I could think of quite a few good reasons, but they were not sufficiently compelling. Plus it sounded like fun.

As a result, Yuri and I were out walking along the Charles by the Hatch Shell again. Or more accurately, I was walking, and Yuri bounced along beside me, clearly enjoying himself.

"We're not really here, right?" he asked.

"I'm not here," I said. "I don't know about you."

"No. I'm not here either. This meeting definitely never happened."

There was just something about Yuri that I always found amusing. Sometimes just looking at him made me laugh.

"What's up this time?" he asked.

I had decided Yuri could probably help me find out what was going on with cardiac surgery at Laurel Hill.

"Incidentally, I'm not supposed to talk to you," Yuri continued. "You probably didn't know that."

"Who told you not to talk to me?"

"Guess who."

"I gather that I know this person?"

"Yes. I think you scare him."

"OK, so I think you must be talking about Glenn Santoro. The jovial detective."

"Yes, Santoro," Yuri said, "but I don't think he's really that jovial. He seemed pretty heavy-duty serious to me."

"What do you think he'd do if he knew we were here like this talking about Laurel Hill?"

"He won't find out. Don't worry about it." Yuri continued to bounce along, clearly oblivious to the threat of any real danger.

"Maybe we should be wearing wigs," I said.

"Gideon, he's just one person. He can't be everywhere. And even if he sees us walking together, big deal. We've been friends since we started college. There is no law that says we can't walk along the river together."

"I guess we just have to make sure he doesn't record what we're saying."

"Gideon, you're getting totally nuts about this. Loosen up."

"You think?"

"Anyway, I think it would be fun to spend a night in jail."

"Yeah right. I'm nuts? Yuri, you're nuts. The last thing you want is to spend a night in jail."

"It's not going to happen."

"OK. Whatever. Listen, Yuri, I have an assignment for you. You want to hear it?"

Yuri smiled at me and sort of chortled.

"I take that for a yes," I said. Yuri just smiled. He was waiting for his assignment. Sort of like a dog waiting for his master to throw a stick out so he could chase it.

Except of course that Yuri was apparently a quasi-nation state, not a dog.

"OK, so tell me what's going on. You are working for Boston Central Health System right now, right?"

"Yes. I got my division attached to the team at IntelliSciTech that works for the health system. This whole thing has spiraled way out of their league. They need my division to help figure it out for them. There's no way they could do it themselves. They don't have the expertise."

"What expertise?"

"Gideon, you know I can't tell you that." Yuri laughed as he said that. He was jerking my chain. I could probably get him to tell me more, but what was the point? I really had no need to know.

"OK, Yuri, but what are they asking you to do? I assume you can tell me that."

"It's mostly the two emails. We are supposed to figure out what happened. Who did it."

"You can do that?"

"I really don't know what we'll find. Of course, you already told me who did it. It was this Vikram guy who is now in India. Apparently, he took the hard drive out of his computer when he left. He replaced the local router too. You managed to get him totally freaked out, Gideon. You got him going completely batshit."

"I rattled his cage."

"You sure did."

"You told me to."

"I know."

"But, Yuri, the hard drive must be all backed up."

"The files are all backed up. But that's just the work he was doing. Yes, of course, they still have that. It's all the little footprints that he took. Deleted files. Deleted websites that he visited. Things we could have recovered."

"What will your group do?"

"Oh, we can do a whole lot of things. We'll sift through all the Laurel Hill and Boston Central networks. We'll probably want to cross-tabulate that with a whole bunch of national network traffic. That will be a huge amount of data, but we should be able to pull something coherent out of it. It will definitely help that I already basically know what happened. About Vikram."

"How do you get the national network traffic?"

Yuri looked at me and smiled.

"Wherever," he chuckled.

That was clearly all he was going to say. It was enough. Nation-states must squirrel all that stuff away on absolutely huge server farms.

"What's my assignment? Come on, Gideon. I need to know."

I told Yuri all about the Laurel Hill cardiac image database. About how Arnold found out about it. And all the stuff Rachael told me. When I mentioned the IT consulting firm that Arnold had hired to figure out what happened, Yuri perked up.

"I know a couple of people there really well," he said. "OK, I'll have to think of some way to tuck all this into our investigation of the emails. That shouldn't be too hard. If necessary, we can add some suspicious-looking links ourselves and then 'discover' them. No big deal."

"I'll leave all that to you guys," I said.

"The only real problem right now is the senator," Yuri said. "There are now three separate federal agencies each trying to investigate this thing. And that is all because of the senator."

"What three?"

"Well, first of course there's the FBI. But the senator also insisted that people come up from the Justice Department cybersecurity unit and from the Homeland Security cyber-crimes unit. They all got sort of tossed in a heap on top of this thing."

"What are they doing?" I asked. "I mean, what are their roles?"

"Who knows? They are supposed to coordinate."

"Good luck on that."

"Exactly. Virtually nothing is being accomplished. Officially, that is. That's of course not counting all the stuff IntelliSciTech is doing that we're not telling them about."

"You can do that?"

"Gideon, we're working on so many different projects, who can tell? And as far as those three agencies are concerned, none of them fully understand what we do anyway."

"It's easy to just do whatever you want?"

"Anything for a friend."

"Thanks, Yuri. That's great."

Sort of scary too, of course.

"I'll let you know whenever we find anything," Yuri said. "If you get a text from somewhere that says *bingo*, that will be me. Go somewhere and give me a call."

He thought for a moment.

"Gideon, you really should tell me what you're going to do with this stuff when I give it to you."

"Do with it? What do you mean?"

"I mean, it's all coming out, right?"

"Oh, yes. I absolutely want to blast it all out there. Make it public."

"The media."

"Yes, the media."

"OK. That's important to know. I'll have to be careful how we look for this stuff. We can't leave any footprints of our own."

"Is that OK?"

"That's fine. No problem. But it's useful to know ahead of time."

"You're sure?"

"Gideon, if this is what you want, this is what you'll get."

Helping your friends when they were in trouble—that's what life was all about.

30

It would have been nice if I could put an alert in The Boston World website so that it automatically emailed me any articles about Laurel Hill Hospital. But that would clearly have risked blowing my covert role.

Instead, I bought an actual paper from one of those little white boxes on sidewalks, the kind you put actual quarters into. It was like using a pay phone instead of my cell. A blast from the past. I wonder how many pay phones were left in America today compared to twenty-five years ago. Ten percent? Probably not even that. But I digress.

I inserted my quarters, extracted an actual paper, and flipped through the pages looking at the titles of articles. I found it on the front page of the Metro section. That was good enough, at least for now. The title of the article announced, "Suspect in Laurel Hill Community Hospital Email Spoof Flies to India."

The story followed:

Officials at Laurel Hill Community Hospital report that Vikram Sastri, PhD, a computer scientist whom they strongly suspect of authoring two spoofed emails discussing the recent suspected murder of Dr. James Arnold, has apparently fled to India. Dr. Sastri was working as a computer consultant at the hospital and is reportedly a highly skilled computer programmer . . .

The story went on to describe the two emails in general terms. It described the attachment on the second email using terms like "a gross violation of patient privacy" and "a clearly illegal breech of confidential patient data." It said that the two spoofed emails were made to look like they came from members of the medical staff but did not mention any names in that regard. In particular, it did not mention my name.

Thank you, Gwen. Thank you very much for that.

It then attempted to describe how complex and sophisticated the task of spoofing those emails must have been. It also mentioned that the motive for sending them was unclear.

The article then launched into a description of how a web search had uncovered the engagement announcement and how that announcement had tied Vikram to Namrata, who was described as a Laurel Hill Hospital anesthesiologist known to be extremely upset about the takeover of Laurel Hill by the health system.

It described how the reporter had called Vikram requesting an interview to discuss the two emails, and how just ten hours after that phone call, the two lovebirds had been on a jet plane to India. And that they had indicated their intention to stay there permanently. And that they had left virtually all their US possessions behind.

It then described how an initial investigation discovered that some equipment, including the hard drive, had been removed from Vikram's computer, and how a full-scale investigation was underway.

An accompanying article described various sorts of misbehavior that had become popular, including spoofing, phishing, and spear-phishing, and similar fun things that hackers and computer criminals could do these days with computers.

All in all, Gwen clearly had a field day. She managed to write it without any mention of my role in finding the engagement announcement, which was of course totally fine with me. In fact, I thought it was great. The last thing I wanted was for anyone to know that I was involved. But I did want it to come out, and here it was, prominently featured in *The Boston World*.

I hoped Gwen was pleased too.

I couldn't find a ruler, so I took a piece of paper (eight and a half by eleven inches) and used it to measure how many inches of story she had published. Forty-six inches total in the two stories.

Measuring a newspaper story in inches was the Stone Age equivalent of doing a word count, which I obviously couldn't do since I was reading an actual paper. Unless I wanted to count each word myself. Forty-six inches sounded pretty good to me. I assumed this meant that Gwen would be eager to continue our rendezvous in the parking garage. There would definitely be more to come.

31

It took Ben Clarke a couple of days to get back to me. I had stopped by his office, but no luck. He wasn't there and nobody seemed to know when he'd be back. So, I left another message on his cell phone. I was getting pretty frustrated. I really wanted to talk to him.

When Ben finally called, it was late morning and I was doing electronic paperwork at my desk at Boston Central. We agreed that I would stop by his office right after lunch. When I got there, I was happy to see that Ben was alone. I had told him that I didn't think Santoro should be included. This was just about Laurel Hill Hospital.

Ben was clearly mystified when I started leading him along a series of hospital corridors without telling him where we were going. I had already called Rachael and she was waiting to talk to us.

"I have someone you need to talk to," I said.

"Who's that?"

"I'm not supposed to tell you until we get there." I was having fun.

"Does this mean you are continuing to investigate Arnold's murder?" he asked as we went up a staircase and continued along another corridor. "Santoro will be very upset if you're still doing that. I don't want you to do any more of that either."

"This is someone I talked to last week. That was before I talked to you and Santoro. It turned out she has some more information. I am putting her in touch with you. After that I'm out of it."

He looked a little dubious.

"Look, you gave me your card," I said. "You told me to call you anytime. So I did. I'm actually doing you a big favor. Once you hear what this is all about, I'm sure you'll agree it's something you need to know about. But I'm not sure whether it has anything to do with Arnold's murder. It may not."

"OK. But I have to tell you—Santoro's watching you. I'd be very careful if I were you."

"I am not sure you want to get Santoro involved in this at all."

"Why is that?"

"You'll see what I mean."

"You said *she*. This is a woman you want me to talk to?"

"You'll see. We're almost there."

We arrived at Rachael's office and I walked in first and stepped to the side. I wanted the two of them to talk directly to each other. I had decided my role should be to introduce them and help get things started. Then I would step back.

Rachael had clearly been waiting and stood to greet Ben with a handshake.

"Rachael Ward."

"Ben Clarke."

There was a brief pause. Rachael didn't seem to know exactly where to start.

"Gideon says you're a lawyer here at Laurel Hill," she finally said.

"Yes. I work in risk management."

"That's what Gideon said."

There was another pause. This time Ben spoke.

"When adverse clinical events occur, our job is to protect the hospital and the people who work here."

"Like when patients sue?"

"Definitely when patients sue. But also if we think there's any chance they might sue sometime in the future. Basically, we wind up having to keep track of all major adverse events."

"Risk management, huh? Well, I guess it's what I need. But I'm afraid I have a somewhat different kind of risk for you to manage than what you're used to. But Gideon is right. I think you're the person I need to talk to."

"The sign on your door says Quality Assurance," Ben said.

"Yes. I do all sorts of different analyses of quality of care. I used to do nursing, but that was years ago. Most of what I do now involves computers." She gestured toward the two large computer screens set up on her desk.

"And now you have a problem."

"I do. I have a big problem. I assume Gideon has told you about it."

"No. Gideon told me absolutely nothing at all. I didn't even know who I was coming to meet until I walked in your door."

Rachael smiled. She seemed pleased that I had followed instructions.

At that point there was another pause and we looked at each other expectantly. I wanted to let Rachael do most of the talking, and Ben seemed to sense this. But Rachael clearly didn't know where to start. I finally decided I had to break the ice.

"Before Arnold died, he asked Rachael to look into a database they have here containing cardiac images, angiograms. Rachael can tell you exactly why Arnold got interested in that. It was by looking at his own chart. She can show it to you on the computer. It turns out that somebody has been putting phony images into the database. Replacing the real ones."

Ben was looking at me now. "Why would somebody do that?"

"Maybe because they were doing coronary artery bypass surgery on patients who didn't really need it and they were trying to cover it up?"

"You're telling me that somebody's been altering the patient record?"

"Yes, exactly."

"That's not good. In fact, that's terrible. Even if you make a major medical error, you absolutely cannot change the patient record. Juries will crucify you for doing that."

"Well, that's definitely what somebody did," I said. I looked at him with a bit of a smile. "So, I guess you agree we need risk management?"

"Oh my God." He paused for a moment, probably processing all this, and then asked, "How many patients?"

"Hundreds," I said.

"Somebody altered the medical record for hundreds of patients?"

"We're pretty sure." I paused. "Actually that's not true. We are sure. They absolutely did it."

"And somebody did this deliberately?"

"It had to be deliberate. They made multiple copies of a whole bunch of images and changed the patient-identifying data in each image file. Then they substituted those images into different patients' medical records. There is no way that could happen by accident."

I stopped. I was talking much too much. I gestured toward Rachael's computer screens again.

"Let Rachael show you how Arnold found out about this. Arnold did it by looking at his own angiogram."

Rachael sat at her desk and pulled up a chair for Ben. He sat next to her and she started showing him the same two images that she had previously shown me.

She had to explain things in a bit more detail to Ben, since Ben didn't have a medical background. But he'd been working on medical issues long enough to get the gist of what Rachael was saying pretty quickly.

As they talked, I idly looked at all the memorabilia and photographs on display on Rachael's bookshelves and the walls of her office. A lot of it focused on softball, which had clearly played a big role in her life. There were various team pictures and trophies, including several MVP awards.

There was also a small photo album. As I leafed through it, a picture caught my eye. It showed two young women dressed as nurses, surrounded by what looked like a group of friends and family members. One of the women was clearly Rachael. The woman standing next to her, a girl really, was considerably younger. She appeared to be holding up a diploma. She was probably just graduating from college with her nursing degree. *A graduation picture.*

The younger woman had the same lanky build as Rachael and the same ponytail but didn't look particularly similar. There was maybe a vague family resemblance at best.

"Is this your sister?" I asked, somewhat abruptly interrupting her discussion with Ben.

Rachael looked up, a bit annoyed and distracted.

"Yes," she said. "That's Ellie Hayes. My half sister." Then, barely glancing at me, she turned back to Ben.

As I watched her, I got a funny feeling. There was something strange about Rachael's tone. She sounded stressed by my question. I thought about it for a minute or so and then decided to press further.

"Your sister works at Laurel Hill Hospital too?"

Rachael turned, clearly annoyed. I was interrupting her a second time. People with ADD tended to interrupt a lot. Occasionally it worked to my advantage.

"She used to work here. Yes. Anything else?"

I let her get started again with Ben. I waited a couple of sentences and then interrupted a third time.

"She works somewhere else now?"

At this point, Rachael was looking quite distracted and disturbed. It was the first time I had ever seen that "deer in the headlights" look that people talk about. She paused. There were maybe fifteen seconds of silence.

"My sister committed suicide two years ago," she finally said.

Our eyes locked, and Rachael looked angry. I remembered what I had heard about a nurse committing suicide after having an affair with Arnold.

I had no idea what kind of expression I was projecting. Probably stunned surprise. I stood there in total shock. I suddenly knew who had killed Arnold and why. I was looking directly at the murderer. And the murderer was looking directly at me.

And she knew that I knew.

Ben continued to look at the two images of Arnold's heart, completely oblivious to our little drama.

I turned and looked back at one of Rachael's bookcases. At this point, my brain was vibrating, and I was not focused on anything I was looking at.

There was a period of silence that seemed to last forever, but which probably lasted for thirty seconds or so. Then Rachael continued her explanation of what Arnold discovered.

Meanwhile, I continued pretending to look at the bookcase.

I tried to process what had just happened without much success. I finally figured out what I needed to do.

Retreat.

I walked toward the door. I did my best to formulate a couple of coherent sentences. "I'll leave you two to continue this discussion. And, Ben, don't forget to ask Rachael about the consultants who have been analyzing all this for her."

Ben looked up. "That's fine, Gideon. We're good here. And thank you very much for setting this up. This is obviously a complete disaster. It needs to be dealt with very quickly."

I nodded back at him and headed out the door. I didn't even try to say anything to Rachael. What was there to say?

As soon as I got out the door, I walked quickly to the end of the long hallway and around the corner. Then I stopped and tried to collect my thoughts. At this point I had no idea where I was going. I mainly just wanted to get out of that office and out of sight. I took a few breaths. I decided to go to my car and get completely out of there.

32

What the hell do you do in a situation like this? I asked myself that question over and over all day long, and I still didn't have any kind of reasonable answer.

I knew who had killed Arnold—and why. But there didn't seem to be any way I could ever prove it. Locking eyes with the killer and knowing what had happened sure didn't count as proof, and that was all I had.

You'd think I would have doubts, that maybe I was reading much too much into that whole interaction with Rachael. But I was morally certain Rachael had switched that syringe and killed Arnold.

As I continued to think about all this, a funny thing happened. I started thinking about sleeping dogs. In particular, I started thinking about letting sleeping dogs lie.

And why not? Why not let sleeping dogs lie? After all, Arnold was indisputably a total asshole. His complete and utter callousness had driven Rachael's sister to commit suicide. And for that Rachael took revenge.

If there was any way to actually prove my theory, then Rachael should be tried and punished. You weren't supposed to kill people—not even total assholes. But what if it was impossible to prove? And so what if she got away with it? Was offing Arnold really such a terrible thing? She was, in a sense, a vigilante.

Yay, Rachael! Go girl!

I really couldn't figure out what to do, and I needed someone to talk to. Who better than my trusted wife?

That evening after the kids had gone to bed, Lucy and I were out on our deck, breathing the summer air and watching the stars through the trees.

"Hey," I said. "Is this a good time to talk? I have a question."

"Uh-oh. You've got that gleam in your eye again. What is it this time? And do I really want to know?" There must have been something about the tone of my voice that she was picking up on.

"I need help," I said.

"What's the question?"

"Well, actually it's a hypothetical situation. Not so hypothetical really. Here it is. Suppose you were working quite closely with a man, a colleague, over a period of couple of months."

"OK."

"And suppose you know that this man had seduced your younger sister."

"OK."

"And suppose that he did this sort of thing all the time. And that he was a real cold, calculating prick about it."

"OK. Why do I think there's more to come?"

"Oh, there's definitely more. Suppose that this guy was such a prick that your sister jumped off a ten-story building and killed herself."

"Gideon! Come on!" Lucy sat up in her deck chair and twisted around so she could look at me. "Why am I working with this guy? And why is he working with me? For crying out loud. I'd kick his nuts in. I'd damn sure never work with him."

"He doesn't know you're her sister. You are actually half sisters. Different last names."

"Are you talking about Arnold? Did Arnold do this?"

"He did. The woman is Rachael Ward. Her sister was a nurse at Laurel Hill who committed suicide two years ago."

"And this all actually happened? Rachael Ward was working with Arnold? On some kind of project? Is this that cardiac surgery thing you were talking about?"

"Yes. Rachael works on quality assurance for Laurel Hill. She used to be a nurse, but now she works with computers."

"And you're sure this happened to her sister?"

"Rachael told me part of it herself, the part about her sister committing suicide. I talked to other people and filled in the rest. Her sister was having an affair with Arnold when she killed herself."

"This is definitely a motive for murder."

"I completely agree. In fact, I'm convinced Rachael did it."

"But working with Arnold for two months on a project? And without Arnold knowing about this? That's not normal. I can't even begin to imagine doing anything like that."

"That's what she did."

"She had motive. But what makes you think she actually did it?"

"I saw it in her eyes."

"You saw it in her eyes?"

"Yes."

"What, there was a little film clip going on in her eyeballs that showed her killing Arnold?"

"No, it wasn't like that."

"Gideon. Come on. This is getting ridiculous. Please. Start over from the beginning and tell me what this is all about."

As she said this, Lucy stood and walked over to the wooden railing of our little deck.

"It's too hot and I'm really sweaty," she announced.

"There's not much breeze tonight," I said.

She pulled off her T-shirt and dropped it onto her deck chair. Then she stood at the railing again with her arms raised way up in the air, letting what breeze there was flow around her.

I told her about the meeting I had with Rachael and Ben. How I'd seen that picture of Rachael with her sister. How I asked Rachael about it and how Rachael had reacted. I told her about the "deer in the headlights."

"A deer in the headlights?"

"People relate to it better when I say it that way."

"I can see you're convinced Rachael did it. And I do respect your instincts."

"Thanks."

"Well, don't thank me yet. I was about to say that your instincts go flying way out into outer space sometimes. You grab a few facts and go charging off in several random directions at once."

She took her socks off and tossed them back through the sliding doors into the living room. Then she grinned at me.

"I mean, nobody ever said your train of thought always stays on the track."

She seemed to be enjoying finding all these different ways of saying the same thing.

"I am sort of a loose cannon sometimes."

"Sometimes? Sometimes?"

"Hey, wait a minute. Who married me? You did. As I recall."

"Yes. And it's definitely an adventure."

"I haven't actually asked my question yet."

"Uh-oh. Maybe I should sit down." She remained standing at the railing. "Fire away."

"OK. Here it is. I know Rachael did it. But I have absolutely no proof."

"That's not a question."

"What do I do? That's the question."

"Do you dare disturb the universe? Is that the question? Like in that poem you like? *The Love Song of J. Alfred Prufrock.*"

Lucy started pulling off her slacks. They got tossed in a heap on the floor. Now she was standing at the railing wearing only a bra and panties.

This was a bit distracting, but I persevered.

"Yes," I said, "that's the question. Do I dare disturb the universe? On the one hand, I could just forget about this and we go on with our lives. Arnold's dead, but who cares?"

Lucy held up a hand to stop me.

"I suddenly realized what this is all about. You are really talking about me, here, aren't you?"

"Yes. If I do nothing, then nothing changes. But if a lot of people start talking about Rachael doing it, then the whole murder gets effectively solved. Even if we can't actually prove a thing."

"And that takes the spotlight off me. Like you said."

"I think it does."

The bra came off next, tossed randomly back over her shoulder. She was still standing at the railing.

"So, you agree?" I asked.

"I guess I do."

"I should do this? Not drop it?"

"Yes. Please do disturb the universe for me."

"OK, but I can't be the person running around accusing Rachael of this," I said. "I'm your husband. It has to be somebody else."

"Who? Not me. That's for sure."

"Well, here's my thought. I'll explain it all to Strier. I'll ask him to take it to Santoro like it's his own idea. Santoro can take it from there."

"So, it's Strier's idea," she said.

"That leaves me totally out of it. What do you think?"

"Devious."

Finally, off came the panties, landing on top of a little lamp on our deck. She was still standing by the railing enjoying the breeze, such as it was.

For some reason I found it increasingly difficult to focus.

A nude goddess stood ten feet away from me. A nude goddess who also happened to be the mother of my children.

"Really?" I was still working at continuing the conversation. "I thought it was pretty straightforward."

"It's devious, Gideon. But it does make sense."

"OK. I'll sleep on it. If it still sounds good in the morning, I'll go ahead and disturb the universe."

But I doubted the universe really cared that much about any of this.

It was more like *Casablanca* and that "hill of beans." Not like Prufrock.

Lucy walked over and sat on my lap. I was still lying back on a flimsy aluminum-frame deck chair. She unbuttoned my shirt and started stroking my chest. Then she started tugging at my belt.

She seemed to be having trouble with it, so I reached down, unbuckled it, and pulled off my pants. I dropped them on the floor. Then I slipped out of my shirt. Lucy took it and tossed it up in the air. It billowed out and sailed over the railing. I'd have to remember to go get it in the morning.

Meanwhile Lucy had pulled off my socks and tossed both of them over the railing as well. Deliberately this time. She was now tugging on my undershorts. A moment later they were sailing out over the railing in pursuit of my shirt and my socks.

She sat back down on my lap. Now there was nothing between us at all.

"You know, Gideon, I have been feeling extremely stressed out lately. Is that something you might be able to help me with?"

"I think it is," I said, "but not on this flimsy deck chair."

We stood, now holding hands, and headed back through the doorway into our little home.

33

"Gideon. I can't believe this is where you really work. What a dump. This place reminds me of those old-fashioned police stations that got built back in the 1950s." Glenn Santoro was looking around my office at Boston Central. He'd seen it before, but I guess it hadn't really registered.

He had called me and told me he wanted to meet me here.

"This is where I work when I'm not seeing patients," I said. "When I'm clinical, I'm downstairs in the ER. That's very state of the art. The rest of the time, I do research and I teach." I gestured around my little office. "This is where I work at my computer. But I do a lot of that at home too."

I wasn't at all sure what Santoro wanted. To tell the truth, I wasn't sure whether he knew himself. Maybe he just wanted to rattle my cage and see what happened.

"What about Laurel Hill Hospital?" he asked. "Will you people here take over the ER there? Like what's happening with anesthesia?"

"I don't know. Not right away. But it doesn't have to be all or nothing. We might slowly become more closely tied. I really have no idea."

"Your wife and Dr. Strier normally work here at Boston Central, right?"

"That's right. In the ORs. They are over at Laurel Hill Hospital temporarily. Strier will probably stay there as chief. Lucy will come back here. She is not a big fan of that place."

I still hadn't figured out why Santoro was here. He sat down. "Been over at Laurel Hill lately?" he asked.

"I was there last week."

"Still trying to figure out who killed Dr. Arnold?"

"I am not trying to be Sherlock Holmes if that's what you mean. You told me to stop. I did what you told me to do. I still think about it. I'd like to find out who did it."

It was really weird that he would show up here now, and especially weird because I couldn't decide what to tell him. On the one hand, I could just blurt out everything that had happened and tell him I was certain Rachael had done it. On the other hand, I really felt I was not the right person to be telling him that. Especially without proof.

I decided to wait him out. So, I just sat there. I did that when I taught, too. Sometimes the only way to get students to ask questions was to ask if they had any, and then just wait a truly uncomfortable amount of time until one of them broke down and asked something. I did it in a friendly way and I sort of made fun of it as I did it.

It felt like Santoro was trying to do the same thing to me. Maybe it was a technique he used.

He was friendly and smiling but silent. I had no problem doing the exact same thing back at him. After a minute or so— that was usually all the time it took—I broke the silence.

"Was there something you wanted to ask me?"

"Yes, Gideon, there is. Something sort of odd is going on with Ben Clarke and I get the feeling you have something to do with it."

"I did talk to Ben last week."

"I thought I told you really clearly to stay out of this."

"You told me to stop investigating, and Ben was sitting right beside you saying the same thing. I stopped. But before I met with you and Ben, I had learned something. Something that is going on at Laurel Hill Hospital. I decided Ben should know about it, so I met with Ben."

"You really need to stay out of this investigation."

"You both told me to let you know if I found anything out. I was following your instructions. I was letting Ben know about something I had already found out."

"Something to do with Dr. Arnold? With the murder?"

"It definitely had to do with Arnold. I had thought it might have something to do with the murder. But now I don't think it's connected with the murder at all."

"What did you tell Ben?"

Now I was really stuck. If the whole business of cardiac images had nothing to do with the murder, I was not so sure I wanted to be telling the police about it.

"It's sort of sensitive."

"This is a murder investigation."

"Can't you just ask Ben?"

Santoro looked at me for a moment. "I am asking you. I want you to tell me about it."

It suddenly hit me what this was all about. Ben wasn't talking. Ben was not telling Santoro anything about the cardiac image database. Ben was trying his best to keep it under wraps. And if he wasn't telling them, it sure wasn't my place to say anything.

"Look, Detective, I'll tell you everything I know if Ben says it's OK. Let's meet with him again. Then you can ask me any questions you want. As long as Ben says it's OK, I'll answer anything."

"That's not the way it works. I am going to ask you questions now. Here. If you refuse to answer, I am going to take you downtown to one of our interrogation rooms. If you can get Ben to join us there, that's fine with me."

It was a bizarre situation. I planned for the whole cardiac image business to come out to the world in the media. With Gwen's help, hopefully in *The Boston World*. I had no problem with that, as long as the leaks couldn't be traced to me. But threats or no threats, I wasn't going to cooperate. It was Ben's job to handle legal stuff. My job was to save lives.

I finally turned to Santoro.

"I don't feel right doing this unless Ben is here. He's our lawyer. If this means we have to go for a ride, let's go for a ride."

I was trying to think how Bogart would say this. Sam Spade.

Santoro looked at me with a big smile and shrugged. I got the feeling he was doing this just to piss me off. And put me in my place.

"Let's go," he said.

I had never been inside a police station before, let alone to be interrogated. I didn't think it was something I was going to tell a whole lot of people about. It would raise too many questions about why I went and what we talked about.

As we drove downtown, I tried to call Ben on his cell phone. It went to voicemail. So, I pulled out the card he had given me. It was still in my wallet. I called his office phone.

I got his receptionist. I introduced myself.

"Hi, is Ben around?"

"Ben is in a meeting."

"Do you know where he is? This is very important. Can you get ahold of him?"

"He's just down the hall. But he's in a meeting."

"Look, I'm in a police car. Detective Santoro is driving me downtown to police headquarters to ask me questions about a conversation I had with Ben."

"With Ben?"

"Yes, he wants to talk about a meeting I had with Ben. I am happy to tell Santoro anything as long as Ben says it's OK. Frankly, I'd feel better if Ben is there."

"Hold on. I'll try and see if I can get Ben on the phone."

Maybe a minute later, Ben was talking to me. I explained again what was going on.

"May I speak to Detective Santoro?" he asked.

I relayed his question to Santoro.

"Sure, he can talk to me. He can talk to me downtown at police headquarters."

I relayed this message back to Ben, who was not pleased.

"What do you think is going on?" he asked.

Basically I thought Santoro was trying to jerk my chain. And jerk Ben's chain at the same time. But no way was I going to say that with Santoro listening.

"You tell me," I said.

Finally Ben caved.

"OK. Tell Santoro I'll be there. Ask him where I should go. Address. Room number. How to get there . . . and don't say a word until I arrive."

"When will you get here?"

"As soon as I can."

The way he said that didn't sound promising.

I spent about two hours sitting alone at a table locked in a tiny little interrogation room with nothing to do. And nothing to read. I guess part of it was intimidation. Part of it was anticipation. I spent most of the time daydreaming about the trip Lucy and I took that summer to Disney World with our kids. I was trying to remember which of the various rides each of us particularly liked. And what each of those rides had been like.

I wondered what real criminals did when they were locked in these little rooms.

It felt like a lot longer than two hours when Santoro and Ben walked into the room and stood at the opposite side of the little table.

"Hi, Gideon. Detective Santoro wants to ask you questions about the conversation we had last week. I told him he should ask me, not you."

"That's fine with me," I said.

They left the room.

Half an hour later I was in a taxi cab going home. Nobody really explained to me what had happened.

But it was pretty clear that Santoro had been putting pressure on Ben to get Ben to talk to him. The fact that Santoro was able to give me a hard time at the same time was just frosting on the cake.

34

had been working in the emergency room at Boston Central Hospital for five hours straight when my cell phone rang. It was eight o'clock in the evening and I had another three hours to go. I was supervising a couple of residents who were about two months out of medical school. They were both pretty smart, but they definitely needed help. Fortunately they seemed willing to ask questions. I always told residents not to worry about asking stupid questions. Being afraid to ask stupid questions was what got people in trouble.

I looked at the number. It was some internal Boston Central Hospital extension that I didn't recognize. Probably some hospitalist up on the floors calling down with a question about one of the patients we had just admitted. Probably pissed off that we didn't have more information about some unfortunate eighty-five-year-old man who had been sent over to us by a nursing home—a patient with five or six major medical problems and hardly any information provided by the nursing home about any of them.

I was prepared to be yelled at, but the call turned out to have nothing to do with medicine. It was Yuri.

"Hi, Gideon. Guess who."

"Yuri!"

"You bet. Guess where I am."

"You're over here talking to people at Boston Central."

"I just finished doing that. I thought maybe I could stop by and see you."

"I'm working in the ER."

"Am I allowed in?"

"Sure."

I told him how to get to the ER from inside the hospital, by the rear door we sent patients through when they got admitted. We'd have to buzz Yuri in.

This would be fun.

A few minutes later, Yuri came tiptoeing out of one of the holding areas full of patients being worked up and evaluated. There were currently seven patients in the holding area, all on stretchers. Light-tan movable drapes partitioned the room, separating the patients from one another. Actually, the drapes were probably beige. I could never remember what color beige actually was. Maybe they were off-white.

But I digress.

Since Yuri had come from inside the hospital, he had wandered through our holding area. For once Yuri wasn't bouncing. In fact, he looked a little tentative and lost.

I waved at him across the central ER nursing station, filled with busy nurses, techs, clerks, and doctors. When Yuri spotted me, he brightened up.

I led him into one of the cardiac rooms that was not being used. It was waiting for the next unstable heart attack patient to arrive at the ER. I pulled a drape most of the way across the doorway and sat on one of the chairs.

Yuri looked at all the computer screens. There was a big one right next to the stretcher where the patient would go, whenever he or she arrived. Yuri went up and stared at it, evidently trying to decipher what was written on the screen.

"This must be the electronic medical record," he said to me, examining it with great interest, "the one you guys hate so much."

"That's it."

He continued looking at it. "It doesn't look so bad."

"You haven't tried using it."

Yuri shrugged and smiled.

"Stupid computer." Now he was talking to the computer screen.

"You got it," I said.

"Maybe I should kick it."

"Go ahead and try. I doubt it will help."

Yuri placed his hand on top of the large computer screen for a few seconds, as if he were communing with it.

"Gideon, I feel your pain."

"OK, OK, Yuri. What's up? Do you have news for me?"

"I do. I do indeed have news."

"Great."

"Not too much on Vikram yet. I'm beginning to get the feeling that he was actually pretty good at covering his tracks. We'll eventually figure out exactly what he did and how he did it. But I doubt we'll be able to extradite him or anything like that."

"No proof you mean?"

"We're doing a massive pattern match against a database that doesn't exist."

"A database that doesn't exist?"

"Yes, we have several of those. Really big databases that don't exist."

"And since they don't exist, nothing you find using them can ever be taken into a courtroom. Is that what you are saying?"

"Exactly. So, it's really great you flushed him out and chased him halfway round the globe. We'll just tell people that we know he did it, but that we can't take it to court because of national security. Everybody will understand that."

"So that basically takes care of Vikram."

"Yup. We have more work to do. But what I just told you is going to be the bottom line."

"What about the cardiac images? Anything more on that?"

"You bet. I found out what happened. But not officially. All I had to do was talk to my friends over at GDB Consulting." It was GDB Consulting who had written that big fat report for Rachael.

"What happened?"

"What happened was that the Laurel Hill cardiac surgery group had a very good programmer working for them. He was a friend of one of the surgeons. He's the person who switched all the images around in the first place. It was supposed to be temporary. Just for a couple of weeks. Then they were going to change it all back. It was all because of the audit. Just like you said."

"So what happened?"

"It all fell apart. It's impossible to find out exactly what happened. But I get the feeling the guy tried to extort a whole bunch of money from the cardiac surgeons. A really whole lot. And they refused to pay."

"They couldn't just bargain him down?"

"Who knows what happened? All we know is it went south. They were probably all yelling and screaming at each other. So they finally fired the guy, who of course couldn't tell anyone about it since he was the person who actually did it."

"But then somebody clearly tried to fix it? And it got all messed up?"

"Yes, someone did something. We don't know who for sure. But one of the cardiac surgeons who used to work there apparently knew some programming. We think maybe it was him."

"What happens now?"

"Gideon, you were right. Ben Clarke is trying to hush it all up. He is trying to pretend that it's just some minor technical problem. His concept seems to be that the database somehow got messed up—who knows why. He just wants someone to straighten it out. Nobody will be the wiser. Life will go on."

"Just one of those little technical glitches that happen from time to time," I said. "You know. *Computers.*"

"Yup. Pesky computers. They get messed up all the time."

"So that's it, huh?"

"That's it as far as Ben Clarke is concerned." Yuri looked at me with a big smile. "But somehow I get the feeling that Ben Clarke may not have the last word on this."

"Whatever gives you that idea?" I asked.

Yuri was still sitting in the chair but somehow managed to bounce up and down as he looked at me. Yuri was back in his element.

"Go get 'em, Gideon."

"*Moi?*" I said with mock surprise.

"Yeah, you, Gideon. Nail 'em to the wall. I want to see this happen."

I really liked Yuri. He made technology fun.

As Yuri got ready to leave, I put my hand on his arm and sat him back down. I was still thinking about Rachael, and I was pretty sure he could help us out there too. If so, now was the time to talk about it.

"So, Yuri," I said, "can I give you another assignment?"

"Sure. Why not?"

"I figured out who killed Arnold. And why."

"You've got to be kidding. Who did it?"

"The problem is I can't prove a thing."

"Who did it?

"Her name is Rachael Ward," I said. "She trained as a nurse but then got a master's degree in informatics and now she's working at Laurel Hill Hospital doing quality assurance."

"Why did she kill Arnold?"

"She had a younger sister who was also a nurse at Laurel Hill Hospital. Arnold apparently used to prey on nurses."

"Arnold preyed on Rachael's sister?"

"Yes, and as a result, she committed suicide. Apparently, he was a real prick."

"Did he prey on Rachael too?"

"I don't think so. I really doubt that."

"You're saying this was retribution."

"Yes."

"So how do you know?"

"I saw it in her eyes."

"What?"

"I saw it in her eyes. Sort of like a deer caught in the headlights."

"Gideon, that's the kind of hard data point that's sure to hold up in court."

"I know. I know. That's the problem."

"You have no evidence at all?"

"None. Well, hardly anything. Lucy saw someone who might have been Rachael near her OR just before it all happened. But Lucy was just glancing down the hall. And Rachael, if it was Rachael, was wearing a surgical mask and a cap."

"That's nothing at all."

"I tell you, though, I know she did it. I saw it in her eyes."

"OK, Gideon. I'm sure you did. So, let me guess. You want me to see if I can find out more."

"Right. My concept is that people don't just suddenly up and decide to murder somebody. Even if they are very pissed off. Remember, I'm talking about premeditated murder. Maybe in the heat of the moment they might. That's different. But not a carefully planned-out murder, which is what this was."

"You want me to see if I can find out something more about Rachael?" Yuri asked. "Like maybe she used to torture small animals when she was a child? Something like that? Is that what you mean?"

"Yeah, but I doubt she ever did that. I mean, Rachael is a very nice woman. I seriously doubt she ever tortured small animals. And even if she did, I have no idea how you could ever find out that kind of thing anyway."

Yuri looked at me with a gleeful smile. "Gideon, is there something you're not telling me here?"

"What do you mean?"

"I mean, you are talking about her like you're maybe a little sweet on her."

"Well, you can forget about that."

"Forget about what, Gideon? You want me to forget about something here? Forget about something that's maybe going on here?"

"No, no, no," I said. "Absolutely nothing's going on. I'm just saying Rachael is a nice woman."

I knew Yuri was just teasing, but I suddenly figured out how to shut him up about all this.

"Maybe you'd like her, Yuri," I said. "She's only about four inches taller than you."

"Of course, you know that's not a problem," he said. I did know that. I had seen Yuri with several women who were considerably taller than he was. Yuri never had a problem about his height.

"OK then, Yuri. If she manages to get away with all this, I'll introduce you. She's smart. She likes computers. She'd appreciate you, Yuri. And you could definitely use some more excitement in your life."

"Excitement like a real live murderer in my bed, you mean?"

"Sounds exciting to me. Don't you think?"

"I think you have gone totally off the deep end, Gideon. But we all knew that a long time ago. So, aside from possibly dating this woman, what is it you actually want me to do?"

"Well, what do you suggest?"

"I could start by carefully examining everything on her desktop PC."

"I assume you would need to get some kind of permission to do that?"

"We already have pretty broad permission from the health network to do whatever we need to do. But I would want to keep this under the radar, at least until I found something. If we find anything, then we can maybe put a virus or something on her PC and make it start spewing out malware. Then we can have somebody take it apart officially and tell everybody what they found."

"OK."

"And, of course, we can do an extensive national cross tabulation. I assume you've already done Google."

"Yes. Nothing there. At least nothing I could see that looked at all suspicious."

"OK. Write down her name. And anything else so I can make sure I have the right person."

"How about her social security number? Her home address and phone number are right out there on the web."

"Great, that's plenty."

"And you'll see some photos of her on the web too, Yuri. See what you think. Attractive . . . smart . . . nice smile . . . soft skin . . . likes computers."

"Gideon, I think you protest too much. You sure there's nothing going on between you two?"

"Nothing at all. She's all yours, Yuri." By this time we were both laughing.

"Gideon, shut up. I can't believe you're trying to fix me up with a murderer."

"An exotic woman, Yuri. Just your type."

"Fine. I can't wait to find out more. Remember, I'll text you *Bingo* if I find anything, and you can call me."

"Right. Bingo. I'll be waiting."

35

I sat at my desk at Boston Central Hospital reading my email. Most of it was junk. But these days I inspected junk email more carefully to make sure I didn't overlook a message from Gwen.

"I thought we should talk," a woman spoke from my doorway.

I looked up.

Rachael Ward had tracked me down, which wasn't easy since I was constantly on the go. She must have gotten ahold of the Boston Central ER faculty schedule to find out when I might be sitting in my office. It was now just after two and I was scheduled to start working downstairs in the ER in an hour. I wondered how many times she had tried to find me.

"Hi, Rachael," I said.

Then I stopped. I couldn't think of what to say next to this attractive murderer standing in my doorway.

Maybe "Good to see you." But I really didn't feel that way at all.

How about "What's up?" But we both already knew the answer to that one. I had figured out that she killed Arnold. That was what was up. That was presumably why she was here.

"Please sit down," I finally said.

Rachael had probably rehearsed what she wanted to say multiple times. But now that she was actually here, words apparently failed her.

Sitting there looking at her, I suddenly realized what she wanted—for me to tell her that it would all be all right, that

Arnold was an asshole and that it was good that he was dead. She wanted me to lie to her and say that I had no idea what had happened. That I had no idea who killed him. We would both know that was a lie, but then we could go on with our lives.

And as we sat there silently and all that was going through my mind, I think Rachael realized that it was not going to happen that way. This was not going to be all shuffled under the rug. And there was nothing she could say that was going to make it all go away.

A sad, resigned expression drifted over her face.

"Lucy is very lucky to have you," she said.

Those were the first words that she spoke since coming into my office. It was hard to imagine that was what she had planned to say. And on my part, this statement was completely unexpected, but the minute she said it, I immediately knew exactly what she meant.

There was probably some parallel universe not too distant from this one where Rachael and I were more than just friends— but not in this universe. And certainly not now. Not after all that had happened. Plus, of course, I already had a wife and family that I loved. But I could relate to what she was saying. I could empathize with her pain. I could respect her as a person. I could admire her as a woman. But she was a murder-committing woman, and that was the bottom line.

What to do?

I didn't want to talk about the murder, that's for sure. I didn't want to talk about Arnold. I didn't want to talk about that episode in her office with Ben when I suddenly realized what she had done.

My spinning mind stopped on the thought of Lucy.

"I have to protect her," I blurted.

Rachael continued to look at me, somewhat solemnly. It was probably only twenty or thirty seconds, but it seemed a lot longer than that. Neither of us spoke.

Then finally she nodded.

After a few more seconds she got up and walked out the door.

36

"Gideon, how the hell am I supposed to know all this stuff?" This was Strier reacting to my brilliant idea. I had finished explaining everything to him, including my proposed role for him in contacting Santoro and telling him that Rachael was the murderer.

He seemed underwhelmed. But at least he was still listening.

I sat in Strier's little office at Laurel Hill. Alan Mason was next door dutifully reading a paperback book. When I walked in, I noticed that Alan now had a small stack of books and magazines on his desk. He looked like he had settled in for the long haul.

"I thought about that," I said. "I printed out several things off the web that you can show to Santoro."

I handed him a manila folder. Strier shuffled aimlessly through the pages. I clearly needed to explain my concept better.

"Let's go through this one page at a time," I said.

I pulled out one of the pages and put it on the table in front of him. The door was closed. I didn't want people hearing this.

The first printout was from one of the local newspapers. It contained a photo almost identical to the one I had seen in Rachael's office.

"Here's a picture of Rachael's sister graduating from nursing school. That's Rachael. That's her sister, obviously. Her name is Ellie Hayes. Ellie is her actual name—it's not short for anything."

Ellie was the one holding the diploma. "And these must be their parents," I continued. "The man must be Rachael's stepfather and Ellie's father. Same mother."

"OK."

I pulled out another page. It was a newspaper article about Ellie's suicide. I guessed it made the paper because she had jumped off a large building near the center of town. The article was not very long. I had also printed out a short obituary. These were from the same local newspaper. There was nothing in them about Arnold.

My next printout was from Laurel Hill Hospital's biweekly newsletter. There was a picture of Arnold and Rachael sitting beside a large computer screen. The article talked up the Laurel Hill cardiac surgery program and how it was likely to be expanded. This was just a few weeks old.

I gave Strier a few minutes to digest it all.

"What do you think?" I asked.

I had some thoughts, but I wanted to see if he came up with any ideas himself. I didn't want to totally push this onto him.

"I guess I need some kind of story, huh?" he said. "I mean, I have actually seen this newsletter sitting around. I could start with that."

"Right. So, you picked it up and saw a picture of Arnold and Rachael. You started reading."

"And then I remembered something."

"Right. And then you remembered something."

"I suddenly remembered Rachael had a younger sister who committed suicide after having an affair with Arnold." Strier blurted this out in one breath, throwing his hands up as if to say, "How does this make any sense?" He looked at me for any reaction. I smiled. He was letting off steam, but I had the feeling he was actually getting his mind around my concept. Then he continued.

"Yeah, right. So how the hell did I remember all that? That's three completely separate pieces of information. And the affair and the suicide happened two years ago, Gideon. That was long before I got here. I've been here less than six months."

"Not a problem," I said.

"Not a problem? Not a problem? How so?"

"Look, it's no big deal. I've only been coming here a couple of weeks and I know all this stuff. Did you go into toilet stall number four in the men's locker room? Did you see the mural?"

"The one of Arnold and the nurse?"

"Are there more?"

"No, there's only one. Definitely only one, but one's enough."

"OK. Well, when I went to look at it, suppose one of the security guards told me about a nurse committing suicide after having an affair with Arnold a couple of years ago."

"Did he tell you that?"

"No, but he might have."

"I don't get it. What's your point?"

"My point is that you could have heard people talking about it somewhere. Like maybe in the locker room. Maybe you didn't even see who was saying it." I looked at him. "Yes?"

"I guess."

"You guess what?"

"Well, I guess that could take care of the affair and the suicide. How did I know it was Rachael's sister?"

"Maybe someone was looking at that picture in the newsletter and said something about Rachael having a sister who killed herself."

"So that's the story?"

"That's *a* story. I'm sure we could come up with a different one. But that's at least one story that would hang together."

"And you would like me to take this story to Santoro."

"Look, I know Rachael killed Arnold. I know in my bones that's what happened. But I can't take that to Santoro myself. Otherwise I would. First of all, I'm Lucy's husband. And second of all, he called me Sherlock Holmes and told me to stop investigating or I'd be in big trouble."

"You're talking about the same time that he called me Dr. Watson and told me the same thing."

"Yeah, but I don't really think he's that concerned about you. You work here. This is your job. Sure, I'm part of the health system, but I don't think he really gets that connection. And I definitely don't work here. From his perspective, I am just nosing around where I don't belong. Also," I continued, "he explicitly told you to get in touch with him if you thought of anything else. If you take this to him, you're just doing what he told you to do."

"Gideon, you're absolutely sure Rachael did this?"

"Absolutely certain."

"A deer in the headlights."

"A deer in the headlights."

"So, I take these printouts to Santoro and tell him that story. Do I go through the whole explanation of how I supposedly came up with this?"

"I would suggest not. Only if he asks. Just start with the facts. You suspect Rachael did it. It was revenge because of her sister's death. And then show him this stuff. We should Xerox it first so it doesn't have my fingerprints all over it. Look at it this way. If Rachael did this, Santoro should be told. And once he starts looking into it, he might actually find something out. Maybe there is some kind of proof somewhere."

Strier appeared to be accepting my plan.

"There's one more thing," I continued.

"What's that?"

"The mysterious figure that Lucy saw down the hall near her OR the day it happened."

"The figure that was definitely not Namrata, you mean?"

"Yes. It might have been Rachael."

"Oh my God. You really think so? Same build?"

"Same build. Tall. Thin. Female."

"Maybe it was her."

"Exactly."

"And I could mention this to Santoro."

"Why not?"

"He's going to start nosing around," Strier said thoughtfully.

"That's what we want."

"People are going to figure out what he is doing."

"Good."

"People are going to start rumors that maybe Rachael did it."

"Good. She did do it."

"According to you."

"She did it."

"Assuming you're right and assuming Santoro does go around investigating this and getting people thinking maybe Rachael did it, that will probably help settle this place down."

"Even without proof."

"Right. Even if he can't find any proof."

He thought for a moment.

"This is sort of sneaky, Gideon. But you're absolutely sure she did it?"

"I am absolutely positive."

"She sure had motive." He looked at me and then shrugged. "OK, I guess I should do this."

37

"'m not an idiot, Gideon," Santoro said.

He had returned to my office at Boston Central Hospital. I had come in specifically to meet with him, at his request.

"I never said you were," I said.

"Hank Strier came to me with a theory he has as to who killed Dr. Arnold. You know anything about that?" he asked.

"You're talking about Rachael now, right? Rachael Ward."

"That's right. Strier says he thinks she did it. What do you think?"

It was beginning to look like my brilliant idea of having Strier contact Santoro hadn't worked that well. I was being sucked in and wasn't sure what to say. I decided I might as well just play it straight and hope for the best. At worst I was probably facing another ride downtown. Big deal.

"I think Strier's theory is worth investigating," I said, "and to answer your first question, yes, I did know about his theory. He discussed it with me. We agreed that he should talk to you about it."

"Gideon, I don't think Strier came up with that theory all by himself. I think someone else did. Then that other person fed it to Strier and Strier fed it to me."

"What makes you think that?"

"Come on, Gideon, do you really think I'm some kind of idiot?"

I had already answered that.

"No. You are definitely not an idiot."

I guess I was the idiot.

"For one thing, Gideon, it was all too pat. The way Strier told it to me, it was like he was reading it out of a book. Hank Strier is a bad actor and lousy liar."

"Why do you say he was lying? He believes Rachael probably did it. He sincerely believes you should look into it. Investigate. Whatever. Strier would never accuse someone of murder if he didn't believe it."

"That's not what I meant, Gideon."

"But it is true."

"Listen, Gideon. Like I said before, I am not an idiot."

"OK."

"You know what I'm talking about."

"I'm beginning to think that maybe we're talking about another trip downtown to police headquarters."

"I hope not, Gideon. I sincerely hope that it does not come to that."

"What, then?"

"How about this? Strier told me an interesting theory. I am willing to believe he thinks it may be true. I am willing to believe he thinks I should look into it. But no way do I get the feeling he's totally convinced that Rachael is the murderer."

"There's certainly no proof. Nobody has any proof."

"That's right," he said.

I was beginning to get discouraged, wondering where this was all going. But now Santoro was actually sort of grinning at me.

"I asked Hank Strier a lot of questions about his theory and I actually came away impressed. There's no proof at all—not yet, anyway. But it's by far the best theory anybody has come up with."

"So, you'll investigate?"

"Oh, I'll definitely investigate."

"Good."

"But if I'm going to investigate, I need to know as much about this theory as I can. And that's where you come in."

"How so?"

"Listen, I want to know exactly why you think Rachael Ward

killed Dr. Arnold. If I am going to investigate this, I need as much information as possible before I start. And I want to get it firsthand, not second."

"What do you want from me?"

"Give me a step-by-step description of the reasoning process that mind of yours went through and how you came to this conclusion. I already asked Strier to do this and he was very unconvincing."

"You mean he couldn't convince you that Rachael did it?"

"No, he couldn't convince me that he was the person who came up with the theory."

"Does that mean Strier's in trouble?"

"Not if you cooperate, Gideon. Look, I can take you downtown again if I have to. But what's the point? Why don't you just talk to me?"

I couldn't really think of any reason not to tell him the whole story about Rachael.

"OK," I said.

"OK what?"

"OK, I'll tell you. There's not a whole lot more than you already know."

I told him about the meeting with Rachael and Ben, but I didn't tell him anything about what we actually talked about. I told him he'd have to ask Ben about that.

I told him about the picture of Ellie's graduation. About the deer in the headlights. And how I had left the room totally convinced Rachael had done it.

Santoro asked me a lot of questions. Finally, he seemed satisfied that there was nothing more I had to tell him.

"OK, Gideon. So now tell me why you didn't come to me yourself with this. You knew about this when I had you downtown in the interrogation room, for crying out loud."

"You never asked me anything about this. But more to the point, I hadn't gotten my mind around what to do with it. I mean, yes, I believed she had done it, but I didn't think it could ever be proven. I wasn't sure I shouldn't just let sleeping dogs lie."

It was hard to know what Santoro thought of this. But at least he seemed to buy it.

"Can I ask you a question?"

"Go ahead," he said.

"When you investigate something like this, it's not just looking for information, is it?"

"What do you mean?"

"I mean you are also shaking things up at the same time."

Santoro seemed to understand immediately what I was talking about.

"I see what you're getting at. Yes. We call it 'heat.' "

"Heat?"

"When we're investigating, we're looking for information. But we're also often putting pressure on people at the same time."

"As in turning up the heat?"

"Exactly. As in turning up the heat. And you never know what people will do when you do that. They sometimes do really stupid things. It sometimes really shakes things loose. You never know."

He was talking about rattling cages. It was a different name for the same thing.

"I get it," I said. "I like it."

He smiled. "Why am I not surprised?"

Apparently I continued to amuse him. I decided it was time for me to get back on message.

"OK, well, all I want is to get the spotlight off Lucy. If there's any way I can help with that, please let me know."

"You keep telling me that, Gideon. I'll tell you what. Next time you have something to tell me, bring it to me directly. And watch your step. I'm still watching you. I'm not an idiot, and you're not that clever. So don't try to be. Let me work on this. You do your job and let me do mine."

On that note, we brought our meeting to a close.

Heat. I liked it.

38

I was in the Boston Central Hospital cafeteria eating a quick lunch when I got a ping on my cell phone.

Bingo.

It was a text from an unknown number, but I knew what it was—Yuri asking me to call him. I had a throwaway cell phone in my jacket pocket. I could probably use it safely from the hospital, but I decided to do this right. I went out to my car, drove onto Storrow Drive, continued through the Big Dig into South Boston, and finally pulled up to the curb. Only after doing all this did I attach the battery, slide in the SIM card, and dial Yuri.

He picked up right away.

"Bingo," he greeted me.

"Hi, Yuri. Does this mean you have something?"

"Indeed I do," he said. "Guess what Rachael was doing?"

"You found something. Great. What?"

"Rachael was cyberstalking Arnold."

"Cyberstalking?"

"We found a PDF on Rachael's Laurel Hill computer with all Arnold's web accounts and passwords. She must have copied the list somehow and scanned it in."

"You know, Yuri, it's not really that surprising. She was working with Arnold for two months. All that time she knew he had driven her sister to suicide. Cyberstalking may just be the tip of the iceberg."

"Well, Gideon, since she wound up killing him, clearly it was. And we may discover more. But think about it. This definitely points a big red arrow directly at Rachael that anyone can relate to. Even if we still can't prove she killed him, this goes a huge way toward putting the spotlight directly on her. And completely off Lucy."

"I agree. This is great," I said. This really was great.

"We also looked at her web log. She has been logging into all his websites on a regular basis for the past two months. His email. His personal bank account. His schedule. Everything you can imagine."

"Amazing."

"Yes. Pretty neat, huh? Not proof she murdered him. But definitely not normal. And definitely illegal."

"You mean she went to all those sites and didn't delete the web log on her PC?"

"Gideon, don't be an idiot. Of course she deleted it all. But it's all still there. Just because you delete something doesn't mean it's gone. And it's still sitting out there in cyberspace anyway."

"That's assuming someone keeps track of every website everybody ever logs onto."

Yuri laughed.

"Yuri, you're laughing at me." This must be one of those databases Yuri talked about that didn't exist. But that he used all the time. "What now?" I asked.

"Well, Gideon, now you have to tell me what you want me to do. Nobody else knows anything about this. Just you and me. You want some other people to know about this?"

"Yes. Particularly the detective. Glenn Santoro. But I don't want you talking to him. He knows about you and me. This can't be connected to me in any way."

"Don't worry. I'm not stupid. I wouldn't do anything like that. We'll just put a virus on her machine. Once it starts spewing stuff out, we'll notify the Boston Central Hospital IT people and have them investigate. We'll make sure they find all the cyberstalking stuff that's on her PC, even the deleted stuff, and we'll make sure they give it all to Santoro. But I'll keep myself totally behind the scenes. Nobody will know I had anything to do with this at all. Santoro won't suspect a thing."

"Yuri, this is great. You are a fine friend indeed. I wish I could do something to pay you back for all this. You sure you don't want a date with Rachael?"

"You mean after she gets out of jail?"

"Well, yeah. I guess there's that."

"Yes, there's definitely that. But, Gideon, thanks a lot for the thought."

"You're very welcome."

"I tell you what. How's this? If Rachael and I ever do go out on a date and if we wind up falling in love, getting married, and having a son, then we'll name him Gideon. What do you think? A name like that deserves to be preserved."

"Yuri, I'm touched. I'm really touched."

I thought we were finished, but Yuri didn't seem ready to hang up. I got the feeling he had something to say but wasn't sure exactly where to start.

"What's up, Yuri?"

"There's more."

"More stuff from Rachael's PC?"

"More stuff, but it's from her home laptop—sitting out there on the internet. Apparently, Rachael kept some kind of diary. I've only got small fragments of it."

"A diary?"

"More like a personal blog. She must keep it on a thumb drive or something. Not online. I found pieces of it sitting in her RAM scratch space. It'll get overwritten pretty quickly as she uses the laptop for other things. But I copied out everything that was there."

"Does she say she killed Arnold?"

"No, at least not in what I have. But we can't tell anyone about this anyway. The technology I used to get it is secret. Want to hear some of it? I can't email it, but I can read it to you on the phone."

"Yes, please. Absolutely."

"OK, here's one part. This is about her sister." He started reading.

I still can't imagine what she saw in Dr. Arnold. She was much too young. Swept off her feet by a charming manipulator. I wish I had known what was going on. I had absolutely no idea until I got that phone call at 4:23 AM and had to drive through the snow to the city morgue. Ellie was a beautiful girl, full of fun and wonder growing into a woman. But you don't look pretty after you've jumped off a ten-story building. I stood there staring at the broken remnants of a living being trying to identify someone I loved. How the hell was I supposed to know if that bloody mess was my sister's face?

Yuri paused.

"Poor Rachael," I said.

"You said it. Poor Rachael. You gotta feel sorry for her. Then a little further on there's this."

Arnold deserved to die. Whatever happens, it was worth it. Fuck you, Arnold. I'm glad you're dead.

"Wow, that's pretty explicit," I said. "But she doesn't actually say she did it. It's not a confession."

"No, it's not a confession. And we could never prove she wrote it anyway. If we went back to her laptop, I'm sure we'd find the whole thing was long gone. Completely overwritten."

"We'd have to find the thumb drive."

"Gideon, we can't tell anybody about this. We'd have to explain how we knew about it, and we can't. This is just between you and me."

"OK."

"There's another part you need to hear, though. It's about you. Listen to this."

I thought I was totally safe. Now I have no idea what's going on. People are running around behind my back saying things. One of the police detectives suddenly started talking to a bunch of Ellie's friends, asking why she killed herself, asking about Dr. Arnold, and asking about me. And now he's talking to my own friends. They're not supposed to tell me what he's asking them about, but they're telling me anyway. And they're all starting to look at me funny.

"Santoro told me he was going to start doing that," I said. "But that's all about Santoro. None of that's about me."

"But right after that there's this. This is the part that's about you."

It's pretty clear who I have to thank for all this. Gideon Lowell. Gideon is dangerous. He doesn't look dangerous, but he is. And now he's trying to throw me under the bus. I didn't see this coming. Well, he won't see me coming either. We'll see who throws who under what bus.

"Uh-oh," I said.

"I agree. You needed to know about this. I have no idea what she's thinking and how serious she might be, but you clearly need to be careful."

"She already killed one person."

"She did. But you know, Gideon, it's funny. The more I read this stuff, the more fascinated I get. And there's quite a bit more. Random thoughts about lots of different things. This is an interesting woman."

I couldn't help laughing.

"You may remember I kept telling you that."

"She has an interesting mind."

"Also a criminal mind."

"True."

"Maybe you have something in common there, Yuri. Kindred souls? What do you think?"

"You think I'll ever get to meet her?"

"I sort of doubt it, Yuri. Why? You want to meet her now?"

"I really feel sorry for her."

"If she knew what you were doing, she'd probably want to throw you under the bus too."

"I like her mind."

"I tell you what. I'll send you a few links to some nice pictures of her."

"I'd like to see them. Yes, please do. And, Gideon, you need to be careful."

"I'll be careful. You take care."

On that note we hung up.

After that I took the battery and SIM card out of the throwaway phone. I used a pair of scissors and cut the SIM card into six little pieces. I put the phone in a paper bag, placed it on the pavement, picked up a heavy stone and smashed it into the phone about twenty times. Then I distributed all the various pieces into multiple trash bins.

Ian Fleming would have been proud of me.

39

was back in the parking garage waiting for Gwen. It was early evening. I was still taking precautions. On my way over, I had headed off into a residential neighborhood and drove randomly around for about ten minutes to make sure nobody was following.

I had also decided that my personal cell phone could be tracked. I tried storing it in the little radio-opaque baggie that had been provided with my E-ZPass transceiver, but it still worked. So I decided to disconnect the battery and SIM card whenever I embarked on these *sub rosa* expeditions.

I arrived ten minutes early and coasted into a parking slot way over on one side of the parking area. I turned the motor off and watched for a while. Three cars came in and two left. A handful of people walked into or out of the mall. There was nothing remotely suspicious going on that I could see.

Gwen's car entered and I moved to a parking space near hers. As I slipped into the passenger seat of her car, she looked very cheerful.

"You look like you are having a lot of fun," I said.

"Yes, indeed. I am definitely having a lot of fun. I've been getting a lot of good stuff."

"That's good to hear." I wasn't sure where to start, and she could clearly see that by my hesitation.

"What's up, Gideon? Something's going on. I can tell."

"I have another job for your magic wand."

She looked a bit surprised at first, but then her smile broadened.

"OK, who do you want to go *poof* this time? Are we talking about cardiac surgery now?"

"Yes, it's them. But I don't want them to disappear. I want them to go *poof* and then suddenly appear. Like out of thin air. And start talking."

"They're not talking?"

"Right now they are trying as hard as they can to hush everything up. They hope it will all go away."

"OK, I guess I get that overall concept. But, Gideon, maybe you could give me some clue as to what this is actually all about."

"Good idea."

I told her all about the cardiac imaging database and how it had been changed. How Arnold had discovered it. What the consultants had found. How Ben was apparently trying to cover it up. And how I initially had thought this might be connected with the murder, but that now I was sure that it wasn't.

I did not tell her about Rachael; that would come later. I'd wait and see what Santoro might come up with. Right now, I wanted Gwen to focus on the cardiac images and not be distracted by anything else.

After we talked about all this for half an hour or so, she suddenly put her pen and notepad down and turned to face me more directly.

"OK, Gideon, now tell me how the magic wand comes into this."

"The magic wand," I said. "OK, the head of cardiac surgery at Laurel Hill is Ian Scott. He must know about all this stuff by now, but he just came to Laurel Hill a year ago, so he was never involved in any of it."

"And Ian Scott is the next target for the magic wand?"

"That's my thought."

"That's Dr. Ian Scott? He's a doctor?"

"He's a cardiac surgeon."

"OK, Gideon. So exactly what do you have in mind here?"

"Well, first of all, how much information do you need to write a story about this? I've told you everything I know. Yuri can confirm a lot of this if you need him to. But both of us would have to be background. You can't use our names. Is that enough for you to write a story? Of course, you may have other sources too."

"I do. Yes, I will call Yuri. I will also call a couple of other people I know. I am pretty sure that will be enough to write a story."

"Would it help to have confirmation from Ian Scott?"

"Absolutely. That would absolutely break this story wide open. If I could do that, this whole thing could easily go national."

"It would be a big scandal."

"It would be a very big scandal."

"OK. So, my concept is this. First you get enough to write the story. Then you call Ian Scott and tell him the story is about to come out. You're really doing him a big favor. It's got to be in Laurel Hill's interest to get out ahead of this. For example, they could tell you that they are working to find out exactly what happened and to do whatever might be necessary to fix everything. You could tell him you know that this all happened before he came here and that he didn't have anything to do with it. Tell him you promise to make that absolutely clear in your story if he'll talk to you about this."

"You basically want me to ambush Ian Scott. That's what you want?"

"Yes. Exactly. That's my idea. Waving your magic wand. What do you think?"

"*Poof,*" she said.

"Yes. *Poof.*"

"OK, Gideon. One way or another this is a great story. And if I can get any kind confirmation from Laurel Hill, that will be even better."

"One more thing," I said.

"What's that? There's more?"

"No. Nothing more. But I brought a present for you. Can you guess what it might be?"

"Tell me."

"You have to guess. Think."

"A bottle of wine?" She ventured. "A cake?"

I opened the small bag I was carrying and took out the wand I had purchased earlier in the day.

"I bought this at a magic store. This way it's official."

She picked it up and waved it around.

"I like it," she said. "This will definitely come in very handy."

"Now you have the real thing."

As I got out of the car, Gwen was still waving the wand with various flourishes. She had a flair for it. She made me think of Mozart conducting a symphony. I guess magic came in different forms.

To each his own. Or her own, as the case may be.

Later that evening I was going through my email when a message came in from a random sender. It was an exact copy of that phishing email I had given to Gwen, ostensibly telling me that my email account would be disconnected if I didn't provide my login information. But really telling me to call Gwen. There was only a single period at the end of the first sentence, which meant that it was not urgent.

But I really wanted to know what she had to tell me. I went downstairs, got into my car, and drove about a mile and a half down Memorial Drive. I pulled into a strip mall parking lot, assembled one of my throwaway cell phones, and called her.

"Hi, Gideon. Guess what."

She sounded cheerful and excited. I thought I knew what that meant.

"It sounds like the magic wand worked," I said.

"*Poof*," was her reply.

"What happened?" I asked.

"Well, at first he tried to blow me off with miscellaneous mumbo jumbo about unnecessary surgery. But thanks to you, I was able to quote several articles back at him. That totally took him by surprise. And at that point I think he realized he had nowhere to run. That I had a story and that I knew what I was talking about."

"He caved in?"

"He told me he'd have to call me back. I made sure he knew that this was all going to happen pretty soon."

"And he called back?"

"Yes, indeed. Within an hour I was sitting in his office talking to him and to that Ben Clarke kid lawyer you told me about. Ben started out trying to tell me that it was just some kind of computer mix-up. But as soon as I told him what I knew, it became pretty clear to him that that wasn't going to work."

"So they caved."

"They caved."

"What happens next?"

"Well, Gideon, I think you're just going to have to read *The Boston World* tomorrow morning."

"OK. I will of course definitely do that."

"And right now I have a whole lot of work to do and no time to do it in. I gotta go."

"Have fun."

40

I stopped by Laurel Hill to talk to Strier the next morning. I had been totally consumed getting the kids off to school and I hadn't had a chance to check *The Boston World* online. I planned to buy an actual paper from one of the metal boxes outside the hospital. But when I went to get one, the box was empty. The paper must have sold out rapidly.

As I walked toward the operating room area, I saw an unusually large number of people dressed in street clothes milling around in the hall outside a large room filled with comfortable sofas and armchairs. A sign on the wall said *Family Waiting Room*. This was where family members could wait while patients were in surgery. Several family groups appeared to be having heated discussions with two men wearing scrubs, presumably surgeons.

Strier was there too, but he was standing well off to one side watching. He had a blank expression. When he saw me walking down the hallway, he subtly gestured for me to join him. I walked up and stood beside him. He reached out, took my forearm, and gently but firmly pulled me down the hall—away from the milling crowd, where one of the men dressed in street clothes was now yelling at one of the surgeons.

"All hell has broken loose," Strier whispered. "Did you read today's paper?"

"I haven't had a chance. What's going on?"

"I have a copy in my office. You should read it. The story's already been picked up on the major national news channels."

"What's been picked up?"

"There's an article about cardiac surgery here at Laurel Hill. It makes it sound like Laurel Hill has been operating on healthy patients and then altering the patient record to make them look sick."

"Really," I ventured, pretending to look surprised.

"I think that's what it says. I started reading the article, but then I got paged to come out here."

"What's happening here? What are these people yelling about?"

"These are the families of two patients who are scheduled to have coronary bypass surgery this morning. The patients are already in the OR."

"And these are the surgeons?"

"Yes, the two surgeons scheduled to do the cases."

I moved a bit back down the hall so I could hear what everyone was saying.

One family member, a man who looked to be in his mid-forties, was grilling one of the surgeons. "Why am I supposed to trust you? How are we supposed to know if my father really needs this surgery?"

The surgeon tried to reply, to no avail.

Another man was yelling, "How much money do they pay you to do this kind of surgery anyway?" He kept asking that but wasn't getting any answer at all.

I had never seen anything remotely like this.

I looked at Strier. There didn't really seem to be a role for him here. And it seemed pretty clear to me that the best thing for him was not to get involved. But Strier seemed transfixed.

This time I took his arm, pulled a bit harder than he had pulled me, and got him out of there.

As we walked back to the ORs, he shook his head as if to clear it.

"Thanks, Gideon. Thanks for pulling me out of there."

"Have you ever seen anything like that in your life?" I asked.

"Never. Never ever. And I have never heard of anything like that happening anywhere else."

As Strier headed back to his office, I went into the locker room, changed into scrubs, and then walked out into the OR suite to join him.

As I approached Strier's office, I noticed that Alan Mason's little office was unoccupied. The light was off, and the door was wide open.

"Where's Alan?" I asked.

"Alan is interviewing for a job. He took vacation leave."

"Good for Alan. Staying in that little room has got to be hard on the soul."

"Yes. It really makes no sense for him to stick around to the bitter end."

We entered Strier's office and he handed me a copy of *The Boston World*. This time we had made the front page of the whole paper: "Laurel Hill Hospital Accused of Covering up Unnecessary Heart Surgery."

The byline read *Gwen Swann*.

Yup, I thought.

I started reading. There was nothing new. It basically summarized the whole situation and was pretty devastating. I could see why the families were upset.

Ian Scott was quoted several times. He was identified as someone who had joined Laurel Hill in the past year and was not involved in the image substitution. Gwen had lived up to her promise there.

In his quotes, Ian clearly attempted to project a calming, responsible image. This was a problem that had just been discovered. Clearly something had happened to one of their databases. They were looking into it and would take whatever action was needed.

It certainly seemed good for the hospital to have his comments as part of the story. But the facts spoke for themselves, and Gwen had spelled them out pretty clearly. There was nothing Ian Scott could say to alter that.

As I read the article, Strier's phone rang. He picked it up and listened for a couple of minutes. Then he hung up and spoke to me.

"All coronary bypass surgery is cancelled."

"For how long?"

"Good question."

He picked up the phone and hit five buttons. Somebody picked up.

"For how long? Just today?" he asked.

He listened and then hung up again.

"Nobody knows. Today for sure. Apparently, Ian Scott, our chief of cardiac surgery, just joined the crowd outside. He decided to cancel the cases."

"What do you think? Will it last longer than just today?"

Strier shrugged.

"What a mess," I said.

"What a mess," he agreed.

I wondered what Ben Clarke was thinking.

He was probably shell-shocked.

41

It was three days since the shit hit the fan.

The day after Gwen's story, Ian Scott tried to get things at least somewhat under control. He personally and very publicly committed himself to reviewing every case scheduled for coronary bypass surgery at Laurel Hill. If he had any questions, he would send the patient to Boston Central for a second opinion. Free of charge.

The following day, however, everything was thrown back into total disarray. The Boston Central Health Network announced that it would be permanently closing down cardiac surgery at Laurel Hill. Other hospitals in the network would expand their services as needed. On the surface, this seemed like a straightforward solution, but I suspected it was not as simple as they made it sound. They would need additional ORs designed for cardiac surgery, additional ICU beds, as well as additional highly specialized staff to expand activities at other hospitals on a continuing basis. You couldn't just snap your fingers and have all that happen overnight.

But the bottom line was pretty clear. Cardiac surgery was dead as a doornail at Laurel Hill. Maybe the network was feeling vulnerable and scared. Maybe they were just pissed off. Maybe Laurel Hill was being punished. Maybe something else. Probably all of the above. They would certainly be sued by flocks of legal vultures already circling.

The media was still hot on the trail of everything that was going on, and Gwen wrote stories about it every day.

As far as Rachael was concerned, I kept hearing rumors. Santoro was running around interviewing people about Rachael's sister and about Rachael herself. I heard this secondhand from Lucy and Strier. Yuri's people would presumably also be passing information about Rachael's cyberstalking to Santoro in the near future, if they hadn't done so already. In some *sub rosa* fashion, of course.

We'd see what developed. In any case, the spotlight was moving off Lucy. Maybe Santoro could get Rachael to explode. Or at least do something stupid.

Heat.

The game was afoot.

42

It was Saturday and I went in to Laurel Hill to have a late morning lunch with Lucy. She was on call and the kids were with our nanny. It was date time. You took what you could get.

My cell phone emitted a sharp ping. A text message from Ben Clarke.

> *Ben: Gideon*
> *Me: Hi*
> *Ben: Can you talk? Just saw you walk in from the parking lot.*
> *Me: I'm in the OR.*
> *Ben: I'll meet you there.*
> *Me: OK*
> *Ben: Outside OR 10 in 20 min?*
> *Me: OK*

The OR area was nearly empty. Lucy was supervising two nurse anesthetists in adjacent ORs. Nothing else was happening. I had changed into scrubs so I could come in and talk to her. I stood in the scrub room as she got everything organized so she could leave the floor briefly for lunch. OR ten was just down the hall.

I told her about Ben's message.

"What do you think he wants?" she asked.

"I have no idea," I said.

"He probably wants to make sure you shut up about cardiac surgery."

"If that's what he wants, I'm happy to shut up," I said, "but it's pretty much out in the open now. If he thinks he can control it somehow, that's fine with me."

I was doing everything I could to make sure it all came out. But I wasn't going to tell anybody about that. Not even Lucy.

Only Gwen and Yuri knew what I was doing.

After a few minutes I wandered out into the main OR corridor and looked down the deserted hallway toward OR ten. Nothing yet. I decided I might as well stay in the hall and wait. A couple of minutes later, I heard the padding of soft paper booties approaching around the corner from me, coming down the hall from the OR locker room. Ben was right on time.

Only it wasn't Ben.

It was Rachael rounding the corner dressed in scrubs and carrying a small green surgical towel folded over. She held a sheet of paper in the other hand.

I was a little dumbfounded to see her there, but she didn't seem a bit surprised to see me.

"Where's Ben?" she said. "He told me to meet him here."

"He told me the same thing," I said. "Ben sent me a text. He didn't say anything about you though. What did he tell you?"

"Ben faxed me this." Rachael gave the sheet of paper a little wave.

"He didn't fax anything to me, just a text saying to meet him. I was down the hall talking to Lucy. She's on call this weekend."

"What do you make of this?" Rachael held out the sheet of paper.

I took it and started to read. It was some kind of complicated legal discussion about the nature of proof. This must be what Ben wanted to talk to us about. I had trouble deciphering the legalese. In fact, I had trouble focusing at all. None of this made sense. And on top of everything else, Rachael was doing something with the towel in her other hand, and rocking back and forth in a funny sort of way.

As I looked at the page and all the legal terms on it, for some reason I started thinking about a book I had read by Johnnie Cochran, OJ Simpson's lawyer. Cochran liked to make up silly rhymes to use in his cases. Like, "If the glove doesn't fit, you must acquit."

As I looked at the fax, I thought of the phrase, *If you ain't got proof, you ain't got poot.* Probably not from the book, but who knows.

I pretended to read from the page in front of me.

"If you ain't got proof, you ain't got poot." I said it out loud this time.

Rachael appeared a bit dumbfounded by my sudden foray into legal reasoning.

"That's right, Gideon," she finally said. "You ain't got no proof at all, and you know it."

OK. What do I say to that?

"All I want to do is get the spotlight off Lucy," I finally said, "proof or no proof."

"You've got nothing, Gideon, so you decided to light a little fire under Santoro, you arrogant asshole."

"Santoro? What's Santoro doing?"

"What's Santoro doing? You know damn well what Santoro's doing, Gideon. Everything. And you set him up to do it. You know you did."

Who, me?

"What's Santoro doing?" I played innocent. At this point, I wasn't sure what was going on with Rachael at all.

"Santoro is talking to everybody who ever knew my sister. He's asking them why she killed herself. He's asking them how I reacted. How I felt about it."

"So, what do they say?"

"Mostly that they had no idea Ellie even had a sister. That it was news to them. Most of her friends knew nothing about me at all. Ellie was six years younger than I was."

"OK."

"So now he's taking all of my friends into a room somewhere and asking them questions, and they're not supposed to tell me what they're talking about. It totally pisses me off, Gideon, and I know this is all your doing."

"Rachael, come on. How does this have anything to do with me?"

"You set it all up, and now Santoro is going around showing people my picture and asking if anyone saw me around the OR the morning Dr. Arnold died. You know anything about that?"

"I had no idea."

This time I really didn't. Clearly this was the heat Santoro had told me about. He couldn't prove anything, so he had turned up the heat and hoped things might shake loose. It really seemed to be working. Rachael was clearly on the verge of losing it.

"Yeah, right," she continued. "I bet. You set that up too. And yesterday he confiscated my PC. Now he's accusing me of cyberstalking Dr. Arnold."

"Cyberstalking?"

"Come on, Gideon, you know exactly what I'm talking about. You set all that up too. I have no idea how you did it, but you did." I got the feeling she might try to punch me out any second. Without warning.

"Rachael—" I didn't know what to say.

"And now you are going to pay!" She looked like a cornered animal getting ready to strike.

Oh my God!

I suddenly realized what was going on. Ben was not coming.

Those texts had not been from Ben; they were from Rachael. She had spoofed the sender somehow so that they appeared to come from Ben.

I backed up, looking for something to fend her off. A cart or something I could hold between us to keep her away from me. There was nothing. But I noticed a fire alarm on the wall. Pulling that would be like hitting a panic button. A fire in a hospital full of sick patients was no joke.

As I was thinking about the alarm, Rachael grabbed my wrist and suddenly moved in right next to me. I felt a sting in my shoulder. Rachael was injecting me with a syringe.

I twisted as violently as I could, and the syringe went spinning out across the corridor. The plunger was only halfway pushed down. The other half of the syringe's contents was presumably injected into me.

If I had any question about that, I found out for sure soon enough. My muscles started to twitch. My legs suddenly felt weak. I knew immediately what it was.

Succinylcholine. A rapid-acting paralyzing drug. A so-called muscle relaxant. Muscle paralyzer was more to the point.

I was being paralyzed.

With my dwindling strength I grabbed Rachael's arm and swung her around. She went flying across the hall and there was a loud *thunk* as her head hit the corner of a large metal equipment cart.

Meanwhile, I sank to the ground. I somehow managed to pull the fire alarm on my way down. A loud shrieking whistle went off and all the emergency lights along the corridor started to strobe.

I sank clumsily to the floor as my remaining strength left my body. As I fell, my right arm got trapped under my body and my head bounced off the tile floor.

My muscles were still twitching. My eyeballs felt like they were trying to pop out of my face. I couldn't move. I couldn't breathe. Out of the corner of my eye, I saw Rachael on the floor ten feet away. A small pool of blood was forming on the floor by her head.

I was awake and alert but completely paralyzed.

As I lay there, I started mentally calculating my chances of survival. If I didn't breathe for five minutes, my brain cells would start to die for lack of oxygen. I tried to remember how long it took for succinylcholine to wear off. I seemed to remember that it took maybe five minutes, a vague residual memory left over from medical school. I had no idea if that was correct. If five minutes was right, then I had maybe a 50 percent chance that some of my brain cells might start to die and a 50 percent chance that all of my brain cells might survive.

Terrific.

The next logical question was how long it would take all my brain cells to die. Ten minutes maybe? Who knew?

As I contemplated my brain cells and their likely fate, I suddenly heard my name being called.

"Gideon!" Lucy screamed as she ran down the corridor. A few seconds later, she was kneeling down beside me. The alarm was still shrieking, and the lights strobed like crazy.

"Gideon, are you OK?" she asked, shaking me. "What's wrong?"

All I could do was blink and wiggle my eyebrows, so I started blinking as fast as I could.

I'm not sure Lucy got my message. For that matter, I'm not sure exactly what my message was, but I was apparently sending her another strong signal due to the fact that my skin was turning blue.

Lucy put a finger on my neck to feel for my pulse. Then she put her lips on mine. With one hand she squeezed my nose shut so hard it really hurt. Then she gave me four strong puffs. I felt my chest rise and fall four times.

She got up and ran back down the hall to her two ORs. Twenty seconds later she was back, accompanied by two surgical nurses, both still wearing latex surgical gloves stained with their patients' blood. Lucy had pulled them right out of their cases.

"Go to the anesthesia workroom and get the portable suction. It's a little cart on wheels. I need it right now!" They ran off and my wife kneeled down next to me. She broke the seal of a bright-orange plastic emergency box that she had put down on the floor.

I felt liquid pouring out of my mouth. My breakfast was coming back up. It was warm and tasted of coffee and scrambled eggs. Lucy had left me on my side, so most of it poured onto the floor.

"Oh shit," I heard her say.

She flipped me over onto my back, put her hand on the back of my head, and pushed it sharply down. My chin was now way up in the air and my mouth was wide open.

I felt a cold metal laryngoscope blade deep down in my throat. Then she pulled up hard to expose my vocal chords.

At this point, I was gagging like crazy and my body was doing its best to thrash around but not succeeding since I still couldn't move. It felt as if my entire breakfast was about to erupt like Mount Vesuvius.

As I gagged and weakly thrashed around, still paralyzed but with tiny amounts of strength starting to return, I felt the stiff plastic endotracheal tube being forced down between my vocal chords and into my trachea.

Talk about something going down the wrong way.

Now I was gagging, coughing, and totally out of control, but still mostly paralyzed. I felt Lucy tape the tube down to my face.

She blew down the tube a few times. Fluid gurgled around inside my chest. Fluid that had managed to get from my stomach down into my lungs. I started to gray out, slowly losing consciousness, fading into oblivion.

Lucy rolled me back onto my side and the rest of my breakfast spewed out around the endotracheal tube all over the floor.

As I slowly faded deeper and deeper into gray, the last words I heard were my darling wife, my life partner, screaming at the top of her lungs.

"GOD DAMN IT. WHERE THE HELL IS THE FUCKING SUCTION?"

43

I could easily have been dead.

Instead, I spent the next week and a half in the Laurel Hill Hospital intensive care unit in a drug-induced stupor. When you were a patient in an ICU, even if you weren't heavily sedated, you could get totally disoriented because there were no windows, the lighting stayed pretty much the same twenty-four hours a day, and they tanked you up with all sorts of drugs. You could even slip into full-blown ICU psychosis. That was the official term for it.

Psychosis meant losing touch with reality. Like big hairy spiders could start crawling all over your bed. Or the computer screens might start talking to you. Or you could be floating around in the firmament looking down on your body from outer space.

I didn't remember anything like that. For me, that week and a half was just a gray blur. Every once in a while after that I would think I remembered something that happened. But I never knew if it was a real memory (albeit a very fuzzy one), a hallucination I was having at the time, or a dream that I'd had since then as my mind tried to process and assimilate that whole experience. Which it seemed to try to do late at night when I was asleep.

So, that's about all I could say about that week and a half.

A gray, fuzzy blur.

What I did recall with some clarity was snapping out of my stupor.

"Dr. Lowell. Dr. Lowell. Open your eyes."

Someone was shaking my right arm.

"Gideon. Open your eyes."

The shaking continued.

I opened my eyes. *Where the hell am I?* My mind felt like it was swimming in molasses. I had been having some kind of weird dream. Now I was in some different kind of weird dream. *Who are all these people and what are they doing in this really weird dream?*

I tried to look around. It was difficult to move my head. And when I tried to move my arms, they moved about a foot and then stopped. I realized my arms were loosely tied down. I was in restraints. I slowly began to recognize that this was real, not a dream.

"Great. You're awake." The shaking stopped and I looked to my right. A woman was holding a flexible plastic tube about two feet long and maybe a quarter of an inch in diameter.

"I need to suction you out," she informed me.

After saying this, she immediately passed the flexible tube she was holding down the endotracheal tube that I suddenly realized was sticking out of my mouth. I felt the tip of her tube way down in my lungs vigorously suctioning out mucus and making me cough violently. This delightful experience lasted for maybe thirty seconds.

They say a cold shower is a good way to really wake up in the morning. Having your lungs suctioned out through an endotracheal tube works pretty well too.

Once she was finished with my lungs, she started in on my mouth. She pushed the breathing tube back and forth from one side of my mouth to the other, while she passed the suction tube deep into my throat, and then moved it back and forth and in and out. She seemed to be getting a lot out. She finally stopped.

"That's great," she said. "You're doing really well. How are you feeling?"

I blinked and nodded. There was no way I was going to be able to say anything with a breathing tube stuck down between my vocal chords.

"Great," she said. "Guess what. We have a real treat for you this morning. Your wife is going to pull the tube out."

I nodded again, looking around.

Lucy's head suddenly materialized out of thin air about a foot in front of my face.

"Hi, Gideon," she greeted me cheerfully.

I continued nodding. It was all I could do.

She produced a pair of scissors in her right hand, and with her left hand started pulling at a band of adhesive tape that I could now feel was wrapped around the back of my head. I realized it was holding my breathing tube in place. She pulled the tape away from my right cheek and cut it. A few seconds later, I felt a very strange sensation deep inside my chest. Before I fully realized what was going on, she had pulled the breathing tube completely out and tossed it into a trash bin. The nurse immediately stepped in again with the suction. There was now a lot more residual glop in my mouth. She suctioned it out.

After that I sat there coughing for about twenty seconds, getting rid of the rest of it. I finally looked up.

Everyone was smiling down at me. Lucy, Strier, and three ICU nurses.

"Hey, Gideon. Welcome back."

That was Hank Strier. He was busy untying my arms.

I tried to talk, but all that came out was a frog-like croak. Then I coughed some more. Finally, I managed to emit a coherent word.

"Hi."

I lay looking up at them. By this time I knew where I was. I was in the medical ICU. I looked around the large room as best I could. Each bed was blocked off by white curtains, so I couldn't see much. Nothing seemed to be going on.

"How long have I been here?"

"Eleven days," Lucy said.

"I don't remember much at all. Why eleven days?"

"Gideon, you had severe aspiration pneumonia and major league ARDS. For a while we were afraid you weren't going to make it. We had you on twenty of PEEP for three days. We also had to keep you paralyzed for a while so you wouldn't fight the ventilator."

"I don't remember any of that."

"You were heavily sedated."

"What did you give me?"

"Mostly Valium, lorazepam, and narcotics." Lorazepam was notorious for producing retrograde amnesia. That was probably why I couldn't remember much.

"On top of all that you were getting antibiotics, of course," Lucy said.

"And we were giving you vecuronium around the clock when you were paralyzed." That was Strier. "We made sure they used fresh bottles," he continued. That was a joke.

"Do you remember being on the ventilator paralyzed?" Lucy asked.

"You know, I do have vague fuzzy memories of that."

"Someday you have to tell me what it felt like. I always wanted to know," she said.

"It's all very fuzzy."

"More will come back over the next few weeks."

An orderly approached us rolling a stretcher.

"We are taking you to Seven West," Lucy said. Seven West was a medical floor for stable patients. I was leaving the ICU.

They had me scooch over from the ICU bed onto the stretcher.

I've always loved the verb "to scooch." Patients who are not too sick scooch around from one place to another in hospitals all over America.

They cranked up the head of the stretcher so I was partly sitting up. Then we rolled toward the door and out of the ICU, the orderly behind us, pushing, as Lucy and Strier walked alongside.

44

We went up to the seventh floor and continued down a couple of long corridors. We finally arrived at a hospital room with a single bed in it. They rolled me alongside and I scooched over.

"Hey, I rate a private room!" I didn't expect this. This was great.

"Gideon, Laurel Hill Hospital is treating you with kid gloves," Strier said. "Think about it. A Laurel Hill employee tried to kill you on Laurel Hill premises using Laurel Hill drugs and equipment. Can you imagine how that makes them feel?"

I thought for a minute.

"Vulnerable?" I suggested.

"I think so. Very vulnerable."

This might have potential.

"Maybe I should see if I can get them to bring me a shrimp salad for lunch. Do you think they feel vulnerable enough to do that for me?"

"If you make a big enough fuss, maybe they will." Strier laughed.

Laurel Hill was the only hospital I had ever been in that sometimes had shrimp cocktails in the cafeteria line.

"And a glass of sauvignon blanc."

"We'll let you handle that one yourself," Lucy said.

I was starting to feel almost civilized.

"Eleven days. Wow." I began to process everything that had happened. "The last thing I remember was Rachael sticking a needle into me. And then Lucy running down the hall to rescue me. Did all that really happen?"

"Yes," Lucy said, "all that happened. Rachael's in jail. She is being indicted for attempted murder. The attempted murder of you, Gideon. If you hadn't made it, it would have been murder. She's very lucky there."

"Not as lucky as you are, of course," added Strier.

"Is there enough evidence?" I asked. "To convict her I mean?"

"Evidence is not a problem," Lucy said. "We found her dazed and semiconscious on the floor right next to you. There was a half-full syringe of succinylcholine right there on the floor with her fingerprints all over it. The rest of the succinylcholine was in you. They did a blood test and definitively identified it."

"OK, so they have her for me. What about Arnold?" I asked. "That was murder."

"I don't think they'll ever convict her of that," Strier said. "There is no way to prove anything. Rachael has a lawyer now and she's not talking."

"The police say it sometimes works out this way," Lucy said. "They know someone has committed a crime, but they can't prove it. So, they put pressure on that person. They harass him."

"*Heat*. Detective Santoro calls it heat," Strier said.

"And then they finally get him for something else," Lucy said. "If he hadn't committed the first crime, they would never have put all that heat on him, and he would never have been convicted of anything."

"So that's what happened to Rachael," I said. "Weird."

"Yes, especially when you consider we almost did get her for murder. But not for Arnold's murder. For your murder."

Attempted murder was OK with me.

"What happens to her now?" I asked. "What's the jail time for attempted murder?"

"It's prison time, not jail time, and there's a range," Strier said. "But because we know she killed Arnold, even though we can't prove it, maybe she'll get pretty near the maximum for the attempted murder of you."

It was sort of sad.

"I hope she doesn't get too much. I admire Rachael. She's a decent woman."

"Gideon," Lucy said, looking at me half bemused and half seriously annoyed, "she tried to kill you."

"I know," I said. "I was there. I may be an idiot, but I do notice things like that."

"And she killed Arnold."

"I know that too, of course. I'm the person who figured it out."

They weren't quite hearing me.

"Gideon"—Strier was laughing again—"what is this with Rachael? If I didn't know Lucy so well, I would have to say your taste in women is extremely bizarre."

"She *was* pretty scary when she came at me with that syringe."

"But you still sort of like her, huh?"

"How about this?" I said. "Maybe I could testify that someone else attacked me." I paused for effect. "Actually, I remember it very clearly now. It was a one-armed man who did it. They need to find him. He's probably on the run."

Now they were both laughing.

"OK, Dr. Richard Kimble, whatever you say," Lucy said.

I guessed I'd have to think of something else.

Meanwhile, Lucy pulled something out of her pocket. She held up a small object.

"Look, Gideon. I have a souvenir for you. A memento of the occasion."

I couldn't make out what it was.

"We can have it mounted and keep it somewhere," Lucy said. "On the mantelpiece maybe."

She handed it to me. It looked like a small white stone. I held it up.

"What's this?

"It's your right front incisor."

I put my hand up to my mouth. My top right front tooth was not there. Apparently, I was holding it in my hand. I looked at my wife, who had a strange expression on her face.

"You knocked out my tooth!" I said this quite loudly with mock indignation. *How dare she?*

"I saved your life," she said smiling.

She must have done it when she was intubating me, half paralyzed, gagging, and struggling with her on the floor of the OR corridor. Knocking out a tooth was a well-known complication of endotracheal intubation. And that must have been about as chaotic an intubation as you could ever imagine. What with me on the floor struggling and my stomach contents pouring down into my lungs and out all over the floor, it was amazing that she got the tube in at all.

I turned to Strier. "My wife knocked out my tooth!"

"Your wife saved your life," he said, looking at the tooth bemused.

I turned back to Lucy, who had obviously been looking forward to this little presentation ceremony.

"OK, but please, next time maybe try to do it without knocking out a tooth. What do you think? As a respectful little wifely gesture."

"Next time I'll be a lot more careful. I promise." She nodded politely and smiled.

"You really want to actually mount it?" I asked.

"Some people shoot elk and mount elk heads in their living room."

"You'll have my tooth?"

I thought about that for a couple of moments. I was not sure I needed my tooth on display, but I did think her knocking out my tooth was sort of funny. An event you could tell your grandchildren about. The day Grandma knocked out Grandpa's tooth. But I was at a loss for what to say.

"I love you," I finally said. "I'm so happy I married you." I figured I couldn't get into too much trouble saying that.

Lucy looked at Strier and laughed. "That's Gideon's way of saying he doesn't want it in the living room." She turned to me. "OK, I'll keep it on my bookshelf."

"I do love you," I said.

"I know," she said, looking out into the distance, and then gave me a wink. She was doing her best Han Solo impression. Fortunately, she was not about to be frozen in plasticrete and shipped off across the galaxy.

Strier sat down on the far end of my bed. Normally you didn't do that with patients, but he probably didn't really think of me as a patient.

"You know," he said, "it's really funny the way this all worked out. It's almost as if it was orchestrated."

"What do you mean, 'orchestrated'?" Lucy asked.

"Well, for example, all those articles in *The Boston World*. Those articles really forced everybody's hands. They drove a lot of all this stuff that happened. They broke the whole thing wide open one piece at a time."

I didn't say anything. I just sat there trying my best to look like someone recovering from being on a ventilator for the past week and a half. It wasn't hard to do.

But Lucy was suddenly looking directly at me with a slightly stunned expression. Light had dawned. I had wondered when this might happen, if ever. She suddenly realized that yes, maybe this had indeed all been orchestrated. And maybe her bright-orange TIME OUT card hadn't actually worked that well after all.

There on the hospital bed, I gave her a tiny little wink and blew her a tiny little kiss. Then I silently mouthed the words, "I love you."

"Oh my God," she said very quietly, almost to herself.

Strier looked at her and then back at me. There wasn't much for him to see.

After all, *sub rosa* was *sub rosa*.

Medical Terms

When writing about medicine, an author needs to include at least a few technical terms, or it doesn't sound natural. But when writing fiction, the story line can't come screeching to a halt to explain each of those terms. On the other hand, a lot of readers may have no idea what some of the terms mean. As a result, I am including these brief explanations.

ADD (Attention Deficit Disorder)—Gideon was diagnosed as having ADD (as was the author of this book). ADD is essentially ADHD without the H (hyperactivity). Based on changes made to the psychiatric disease definitions, ADD is now officially referred to as an "inattentive" type of ADHD. The portrayal of ADD in this book touches on certain aspects but is by no means comprehensive—that would be a different book.

ARDS (Acute Respiratory Distress Syndrome)— Severe lung disease involving excess fluid in the tissue of the lung.

Aspiration—A major risk of anesthesia, especially in emergency situations, is that the patient's stomach contents may be regurgitated and then inhaled into the lungs. This

is called aspiration. If enough of this material gets into the lungs, it can result in the patient essentially drowning. In less severe cases, it can result in infection. This is called aspiration pneumonia, which is potentially fatal. To avoid this problem in elective surgery, patients are told not to eat or drink anything for at least eight hours or so prior to surgery. For emergency surgery, there are a number of ways to protect the patient's airway, including special ways of inserting a breathing tube, in an attempt to prevent aspiration.

Cardiopulmonary Bypass—When surgery is performed

on a patient's heart, it is often necessary to stop the heart from beating and to have a machine take over the circulation and oxygenation of the patient's blood. This is called cardiopulmonary bypass. This is accomplished using a fairly large machine that is essentially a pump that temporarily takes over the function of the patient's heart and lungs.

Code—When a patient has a cardiac arrest, cardiopulmonary

resuscitation (CPR) is typically performed unless the patient has specifically requested not to have this done. When CPR is performed in a medical setting, it is often referred to as a "code." This is presumably because back in the dark ages before beepers, cell phones, and texting, hospital loudspeaker systems used to publicly announce something cryptic like "Code Blue" together with a hospital location to let the appropriate staff know that a patient required CPR.

Coronary Artery Bypass Operation— Coronary

arteries are small arteries that run along the outer surface of the heart and supply blood to the heart muscle itself. If these arteries become blocked, the heart muscle tissue that they supply blood to can start to die. This is what causes a heart attack (the technical term is "myocardial infarction" or "MI").

To try to prevent this from happening, surgeons can take, for example, a small piece of a vein from the patient's leg and sew it onto the coronary artery in a way that allows blood to flow around (bypass) an area where the coronary artery is completely or partially blocked.

Extubation–The process of removing a breathing tube that has been inserted into a patient's trachea (windpipe).

Intubation–The process of inserting a breathing tube into a patient's trachea (windpipe) to help that patient breathe and/or to secure and protect the patient's airway. This is often required, for example, when a patient is given general anesthesia (is "put to sleep") or when a patient has severe lung disease.

Muscle Relaxants–Muscle relaxants used in anesthesia are drugs that paralyze a patient's skeletal muscles (but not certain internal muscles such as the heart). Muscle relaxants are frequently used to facilitate surgery, since the patient's muscles will be relaxed instead of tight and the surgeons will therefore have an easier time performing their procedure. Muscle relaxants are also used in anesthesia to facilitate intubation (after a patient is anesthetized), since it facilitates the insertion of a breathing tube into a patient's trachea (windpipe). If a person is given a muscle relaxant while still awake (as happened to Gideon), that person will be unable to move or breathe, but his heart will still beat.

PEEP (Positive End-Expiratory Pressure)–When a patient is intubated and being mechanically ventilated, a machine called a ventilator is forcing gas (e.g., oxygen and nitrogen) into a patient's lungs (inspiration) and then allowing the gas to flow back out (expiration). A variety of ventilator settings control the volume of gas given in each breath, the number of breaths per minute, etc. One such setting is PEEP. Maintaining a level of positive pressure in between breaths (PEEP) can help keep the lungs inflated and can be beneficial in a patient with severe lung disease. PEEP is measured in centimeters of water (cmH2O). Twenty cmH2O of PEEP (which was used with Gideon) is pretty much the highest level used. Such a high level of PEEP involves a number of significant risks.

Succinylcholine–A fast-acting, short-lasting muscle relaxant that is frequently used to facilitate intubation in an emergency situation when it is important to secure and protect a patient's airway very rapidly to prevent aspiration.

Vecuronium–A somewhat slower-acting, longer-lasting muscle relaxant than succinylcholine that is commonly used during surgery.

A Historical Note

All the contemporary characters in this book are fictional. Captain Gideon Lowell, however, is a real historical figure. The following quote is from "Lowell Genealogy" (www.lowell.to/lowellgen/gentext.html).

> *Gideon was a sea captain. He built, owned and commanded his vessels—one was a 'sloupe' of 50 or 60 tons burden. . . . It is probable that in his voyages, the King's revenue was not always considered, nor did he hesitate to run-up aside of and board by force a French or Spanish craft when opportunity arose.*

Notice that in a typically New England understated fashion, the words "smuggler" and "pirate" never appear—the facts are allowed to speak for themselves. In addition to being a fictional ancestor of the protagonist of this book, Captain Gideon is an actual ancestor of the author, whose middle name is Lowell and who is descended from farmer and seafarer Lowells in southern Maine (as is the fictional Gideon).

CPSIA information can be obtained
at www.ICGtesting.com
Printed in the USA
LVHW110729170619
621441LV00007B/60/P